THE CURSED FORTTRESS

THE 72 DEMONS

BOOK SIX

JAMES E. WISHER

SAND HILL PUBLISHING

Edited by: Janie Linn Dullard

Cover art by: Stone Tower Studio

CHAPTER ONE

The slums of Cairo were a labyrinth, a maze, where only the stench remained constant. The combination of human waste, decaying garbage, and sweat clung to Anatoly's clothes like a second skin. He could taste it, feel it in his lungs as he breathed. But he'd visited worse places during his years as a member of the Circle of Sorcery, so he pressed on, determined to reach his contact. Given the amount of time he'd spent hunting the woman down, damned if he was going to arrive late for their meeting.

He glanced around, all his senses, both magical and mundane, alert for danger. The buildings dated back centuries, though time and neglect had worn them down to shells of their former glory. They leaned dangerously over the narrow alleys, casting long shadows that swallowed everything beneath them. Dogs barked from behind rusted metal gates, their eyes reflecting the sunlight with a feral gleam.

Anatoly ignored them and turned down the alley where the information broker said to meet her. Why she wanted to meet in this place in the middle of the day he couldn't begin to guess. During his years gathering information for the Circle, he'd met many strange people in many strange places. An alley in a Cairo slum was pretty normal as these things went.

His footsteps slowed then stopped. There she lay. At least he assumed the body belonged to the information broker. He'd never met her, only spoken with her on the phone. Her body sprawled across the cobblestones, limbs twisted at unnatural angles. Blood pooled around her, thick and dark as tar. Someone had slashed open her throat, revealing white bone beneath torn flesh. The wound looked fresh; the blood had barely begun to coagulate.

Whoever did this might be close. He expanded his awareness. Many life forms called the slums home. He ignored anything too small to be human and still found dozens within his range. Pity he couldn't tell murderers from innocent people.

Anatoly knelt beside her, hands shaking as he patted her down. He found nothing save a burner cellphone, which ended up in his pocket. No ID and nothing that gave a clue about what sort of information she had for him. Hardly a shocking discovery. Prudent people didn't write down the sorts of things they planned to discuss at this meeting.

He straightened as two pairs of figures dressed in black trousers and loose tunics emerged from either end of the alleyway. Matching keffiyeh hid their faces, leaving only dark, glittering eyes visible. The straight, sharp daggers they held out and ready made their intent clear. It seemed her killers hadn't fled the area after all.

Anatoly considered his options. Fighting wasn't his strong suit, but any wizard strong enough to join the Circle could handle four ordinary men. If he could capture one of them, perhaps the killer could provide the information Anatoly needed.

He focused and gathered ether. A paralysis spell lanced out at the strangers. The moment his spell reached them, it fizzled.

The men charged.

Shocked, but only for an instant, Anatoly sent power into his legs. In one swift motion, he leapt, landing with a dull thud on the roof of a three-story apartment building to his right.

Something crunched and a moment later he fell through the rotten roof. Shards of wood bounced off his personal shield, doing him no harm. The dining room table he crashed through, on the other hand, ended up in many pieces.

He clambered to his feet. No one hid in the apartment, thank heaven for small favors. The door burst open and three of the killers slipped inside. Heaven, it seemed, had done all it cared to.

Anatoly's mind raced as he faced off with the men. They spread out, approaching from left, right and center. He backed up, having no desire to end up sandwiched between them.

He lashed out with a telekinetic blast, hoping to catch them off guard. As with his paralysis spell earlier, this one fizzled, confirming that his only hope lay in escaping.

The window behind him beckoned.

Anatoly turned and leapt, shattering glass and splintering wood. He hit the ground hard, but his still-strengthened legs handled the three-story drop without issue. He looked up to find three dark figures glaring down at him.

They didn't immediately follow, which indicated he wasn't facing wizards. Of course that begged the question of how they managed to negate his spells.

He could figure that out later. Right now, he needed to put more distance between himself and his stalkers. If he could find somewhere busy they'd have to call off their pursuit.

Hopefully.

He sprinted down the alley, weaving between piles of trash and other debris. His mind raced, trying to figure out his next move.

The distraction proved costly when the fourth killer emerged from hiding and thrust his dagger at Anatoly.

A lifetime of training in Sambo saved his life. He turned just enough to avoid a vital wound, but the blade still gouged a deep cut in his side, ignoring the powerful magical barrier that constantly surrounded Anatoly.

An instinctive counterblow staggered the killer and broke his grip on the dagger.

Anatoly staunched his wound in passing and ran on, hand pressed to the cut, and the dagger clutched to his side out of sight. Blood leaked through his fingers and his legs wobbled. He needed to get somewhere safe quickly so he could apply healing magic before he bled out.

He staggered on, determined to escape.

Risking a glance back, he found his trail clear of assassins. Not that they'd have any trouble finding him given the blood trail.

Three blocks later his nose drew him to a koshari place called The Crunchy Bowl. Lunchtime had arrived so the restaurant should be busy. He ducked inside, stumbled over to an empty booth, and sat before he fainted. As soon as his butt hit the hard seat he summoned healing energy. The pain receded at once and he blew out a sigh.

While he doubted he could fully heal the wound, he could stop the bleeding.

A dark-skinned girl about thirteen wearing a thin white cotton dress came over and asked, "Can I get you a bowl, sir?"

Before he could answer, she gasped and stared at his bloody side.

"It looks worse than it is," he lied. "A large bowl with spicy chili sauce would be lovely. And a beer if you have some."

The girl ran away to get his order.

He returned to his healing, working at it until she returned to set a steaming bowl of rice and lentils covered with sauce and fried onions in front of him along with a bottle of beer.

"Thank you."

She nodded, seeming unable to speak. He'd probably scarred the poor thing for life. Then again, if she lived in this part of Cairo, maybe not. In any case, he set to eating, eager to restore his strength. Much as he hoped the killers had given up, he didn't believe it for a moment.

Anatoly finished the final swallow of his beer and sighed. His magic had healed the worst of the wound, though he feared it would remain tender for a couple more days or maybe weeks. Given the alternative, he had no intention of complaining.

A few tables away, he noticed the nervous serving girl watching him with wary eyes. He offered a smile, hoping that, despite coming from a balding, middle-aged man, it would come across as friendly rather than creepy.

It must've worked since she hesitantly approached. "Was it good, sir?"

"Very good, thank you." He held up the empty beer bottle. "Would it be possible to get a second?"

"Of course." She took the bottle and hurried away.

Anatoly dug a ten-Euro bill out of his wallet. That would easily cover ten times what the meal cost, but he planned to occupy the table for a little while and didn't want any trouble about it.

When the girl returned, he held out the bill. "I'm just going to rest here for a bit, okay?"

Wide-eyed, she took the money. "Yes, sir. Take all the time you need."

After a final look at his bloody shirt, she darted back toward the kitchen. A subtle glance around the dining room confirmed that only the girl seemed remotely interested in his situation. People in this part of the city quickly learned to mind their own business, a worldview he wholeheartedly approved of.

He took a sip of his beer and shifted his gaze to the dagger lying on the bench beside him. Nothing about the design struck him as remarkable: straight blade, round bronze pommel, slightly upswept guard. A stream of ether passed through it with no trouble. Whatever had disrupted his magic didn't originate from the dagger. He found that both reassuring and concerning since it meant he had no idea what had, in fact, rendered his magic useless.

Now he needed to confirm if his black-clad friends remained in the area. Assuming his magic could locate them at all. Given their resistance, he didn't have especially high confidence.

One way to find out for sure.

He closed his eyes and sent his vision soaring through the ceiling. All sorts of people moved around outside, but none of them looked like the killers. When he'd checked ten blocks in every direction he let the spell fade. Either they'd given up or he couldn't see them with magic. Much as he hoped for the former, he feared the latter had better odds.

He could do nothing about it in any case. Time to report in and see what the boss had to say. Anatoly cast a sound barrier around his booth, got out his phone, and hit her contact number.

Three rings later she said, "What news?"

"Nothing good. My lead is dead, murdered before she could talk to me. I damn near joined her. The men who killed her used daggers and had some way to negate my magic." He gave her a full rundown on what happened. "Anyway, this is bigger than I can handle on my own."

"Are you secure now?" she asked.

"As secure as I can be under the circumstances. What do you want me to do?"

"Stay there and give me the address. I'll have Daisuke join you within the hour. Also, take a picture of the dagger and send it to me. Crystal can research it and I'll see what I can find regarding magic-suppressing abilities. Do you have any other leads?"

"No, only this broker claimed to have intel on Ahmed. Everyone else I spoke to didn't recognize his name or the Spirit Eaters. The orb is an even bigger mystery. I tracked down the former owner and he said he didn't even know it had magical properties, though he was delighted that he sold it before someone decided to kill him and claim the item. The first bit struck me as unlikely, but my spell indicated he didn't lie."

"Okay, good work. Hang tight and stay safe." The boss hung up.

Anatoly took the pictures she wanted and attached them to a text message. With nothing better to do until Daisuke arrived, he settled in to enjoy his beer.

CHAPTER TWO

Vendors shouted and the smell of roasting lamb and cinnamon filled the air as Daisuke worked his way through the crowded Istanbul bazaar. Hundreds of people filled the area and you could find anything imaginable for sale. He hadn't visited the city in years, but everything still matched his memories.

He kept a brisk pace. Ten minutes remained until his rendezvous with the boss's contact. Assuming he didn't run into a cult, major demon, or some other catastrophe, this should be a quick job.

"Then we can get baklava," Ruq said from his place on Daisuke's shoulder.

Daisuke certainly wouldn't argue with that plan. He was about to make a right-hand turn when his phone buzzed. He pulled it out of his pocket and frowned. What could the boss want? He'd left Zurich like five minutes ago after a full briefing. No way did she forget something.

He tapped the button. "What's up, boss?"

"Anatoly's in trouble in Cairo. He needs reinforcements, now."

Daisuke sidestepped an old man pushing a cart piled high with melons. "I'm six blocks out from the meeting. You want me to ditch it?"

"I'll handle Ali. You need to get to Cairo. But first come back to base."

Daisuke's frown deepened but he knew better than to argue when she used that tone. "Alright, I'm on my way."

She disconnected and he stared at his phone. What in the world happened? Anatoly was supposed to be collecting intel on Ahmed and the orb, not doing anything super dangerous.

"What about our baklava?" Ruq asked.

"I'm sure they sell it in Cairo, not that I'm confident we'll have time to go dessert shopping."

He spotted an alcove and ducked into it. A moment later Daisuke entered the shadow paths. Seconds after that he emerged in the pitch-black closet which served as the Circle's teleportation chamber. The slowly darkening runes provided just enough light for him to find the doorknob and push it open.

The boss stood across the hall, arms crossed, a single sheet of paper in her hand. Her grey suit was perfectly crisp and her eyes glowed faintly golden. She seemed pretty calm, which he took as a good sign.

"So, why am I here instead of Cairo?" he asked.

"Are you firearms qualified?"

Of all the things he imagined she might say, that hadn't made his list. "Sure, I can shoot. But it's been a couple years since I had to use a gun. I mean, black lightning is a hell of a lot more effective than lead. What's going on?"

The boss turned for the basement steps and motioned for him to follow. "Walk with me."

As they descended she said, "Anatoly ran into trouble in Cairo. Killers who are magic-resistant."

Daisuke nearly missed a step. "Come again?"

"He said they were armed with daggers, and both a paralysis spell and a telekinetic blast were negated. His physical enhancement spell worked fine but they stabbed him right through his shield."

"Sounds like whatever they're using has a limited range. That's something anyway."

"Precisely." The boss walked right past Crystal's computer room then paused in front of another door Daisuke had never been through.

Inside, weapons gleamed on tables and racks. Rifles, pistols, knives of all sorts, even a couple swords filled the place. The pungent tang of gun oil hung in the air. Not exactly the sort of thing you expected to find in the base of a group called the Circle of Sorcery.

The boss waved him in. "Help yourself."

Right. Daisuke grabbed a semiautomatic pistol, three clips and a shoulder holster. He slid the items into their respective holsters and nodded to himself. If they had to stab him to negate his shield, this would certainly even the odds.

The boss helped him don the holster, cinching it snug. She looked him over and frowned. "A bit conspicuous. One moment."

She grabbed a black sport coat, one of half a dozen on the only clothing rack in the room and held it out. "Try this."

He thrust his arms through the sleeves and shrugged it into place. "A little big, but it'll work. Anything else?"

The boss rattled off an address. "Anatoly's waiting. He

knows all our resources in the city. You two need to figure out what's going on and the sooner the better."

"We'll get it done, boss, don't worry." He took a step toward the door.

She grasped his arm and pulled him toward her so her face was only inches from his. He caught a hint of tobacco smoke when he breathed in. For a second he dared hope for a kiss. Instead she said, "Be careful."

Swallowing his disappointment, he grinned. "You know me, boss."

"Yes, why do you think I'm so worried?" She released his arm and took a step back. "Off you go."

He marched back to the teleportation chamber. Dealing with magic-resistant enemies wasn't going to be a walk in the park.

"When are our jobs ever a walk in the park?" Ruq asked.

"True, but then again, when did we ever have to deal with magicproof killers?"

"As long as they're not bulletproof, who cares?"

Ruq had a point. Hopefully Daisuke's aim was still good.

Once he entered the chamber, a quick walk down the shadow paths brought him to an alley in the Cairo slums. The stench of rotting garbage remained as bad as he remembered. Just once he'd like to show up somewhere with nice gardens and a cute maid to greet him.

He looked around and shook his head. Not a street sign to be found. Well, someone could tell him how to find the place. "Keep a lookout."

Ruq leapt off his shoulder and took to the air. If anyone tried to sneak up on Daisuke they'd be in for a surprise. He and his familiar followed the chatter to a nearby food stand selling kabobs.

Daisuke approached and waved a one-Euro coin at the vendor. "Hey, I'm looking for The Crunchy Bowl. Know it?"

The man's eyes gleamed. "Ah, yes, Effendi. Not far." He swiped the coin and gestured down a side street. "Take the next left, then right at the red door. Can't miss it."

"Thanks." Daisuke hurried away, eager to find his teammate.

Ten minutes later, he spotted the place. It was nothing to get excited about. You could find restaurants like this on every corner in Cairo. He ducked inside and found Anatoly hunched in a rear booth, nursing a beer.

Daisuke slid in across from him. "You look awful."

Anatoly let out a heavy sigh. "Getting stabbed will do that to you. I closed the wound, but I'm not going to be much use in a fight for a couple days. Not that I was much use against those men today."

"The boss filled me in. Any idea how they blocked your magic?"

Anatoly shuddered. "Not a clue. I've never seen anything like it. My spells just... fizzled."

Daisuke shifted and pulled his jacket open so Anatoly could see his holster. "Yeah. If the bastards show up again, we'll see if they're bulletproof. Where'd you leave the information broker?"

"Not far from here." He drained his beer, grabbed a dagger off the seat beside him, and slid out of the booth. "Come on, I'll show you."

They stepped out into the blazing afternoon sun. In this heat the body would deteriorate quickly. Hopefully it remained in good enough shape for him to extract something useful.

Daisuke fell in beside Anatoly. "Can you tell me anything more about the killers?"

Anatoly shook his head. "Not much to tell. They're well-trained. The group moved like a military unit. I saw no guns, just the daggers. It's like they knew they were going to be facing a wizard and bullets would be useless."

"Was the broker a wizard?"

"Not as far as I know. We discussed nothing other than business; where, when, and how much. Lucky for the Circle's coffers I didn't make a down payment."

Daisuke grunted as they turned into the alley. A single body, her head nearly severed, lay on the ground. Didn't look like any of the locals had messed with it yet. Not that it mattered for his purposes.

He pulled his automatic, chambered a round, and handed it to Anatoly. "I'm going to see what I can find out."

Anatoly took the weapon with a curt nod, his gaze already sweeping the alley. He showed no sign of disapproval or distaste, just cold professionalism. In truth, it made a nice change of pace from Helena's usual reaction to his magic.

Now, let's see what she had to say. Daisuke crouched and sent ether into the woman's head. Lucky for him they'd cut her throat instead of blowing her brains out. Necromancy could do a lot of things, but even Daisuke couldn't extract information from a ruined vessel. And speaking of ruined, decay had already set in. Sections of the brain had already rotted too much to access.

Here we go. Her moment of death. That always left a powerful impression.

A hand clamped over her mouth. Pain in her throat as the killer dragged his blade across. Fear. Confusion. Then... nothing. She never even got a look at them. Disappointing.

He poked around some more, following her path to the alley backwards, ending at a dingy apartment above a clothing shop called Lilly's Frocks.

Last but not least, how did she know Ahmed? As soon as the question formed he found another powerful memory, one of her and the late leader of the Spirit Eaters lying in bed together in the apartment.

They'd been lovers. Interesting. They must've parted on bad terms if she planned to sell him out to Anatoly. He kept looking but found no mention of the elemental orb. Not a complete waste, but less than he'd hoped for.

Daisuke withdrew from the broker's mind and stood.

"Find anything?" Anatoly never looked away from the alley.

"Her address. And an interesting tidbit about Ahmed." Daisuke took his pistol back and checked the safety before holstering it beneath his jacket. "Seems our broker was intimately involved with him."

Anatoly arched a brow. "Why would she betray him?"

"I see two possibilities. One, an ugly breakup. I saw no sign of that, but I couldn't access all her memories so who knows. Or two, she knows he's dead and it doesn't matter what she tells us now. Option two is my guess. Come on. Her apartment's about a mile from here. Maybe we'll find some answers."

Anatoly grunted and the two men set out.

They hadn't gone far when Daisuke said, "The boss told me you know all the local contacts. Best call someone to pick up her body."

"I will once we're a little further away. I have no interest in answering questions right now."

Daisuke seconded that. They had enough questions of

their own without messing around with the local cops.

CHAPTER THREE

Angelique sighed as Daisuke retreated back upstairs. It was odd seeing him dressed in a sport coat, but it did serve its purpose of hiding the pistol he'd taken. She hoped he didn't end up needing it.

Magicproof killers, whatever next?

She felt certain he'd be okay and that he'd find Anatoly in one piece. After all, Daisuke had dealt with an elder demon; ordinary humans, even if magic couldn't touch them, didn't begin to compare, right? If she told herself that enough times maybe she'd start believing it. She had a bad feeling about whatever it was they'd run into in Egypt.

Putting Daisuke and the many dangers he faced out of her mind, Angelique crossed the hall and rapped on Crystal's door before stepping into the dimly lit computer room. She glanced around at the humming, buzzing equipment and shook her head. Crystal's collection of gizmos seemed more arcane to her than most of the magic items they dealt with.

At her workstation, Crystal stared at the large central

monitor. A satellite image of the desert with an ancient stone fortress in the middle filled the screen.

"Is that Taba Castle?" Angelique asked.

Crystal yelped and looked back at her. "Please don't sneak up on me like that, boss."

"I knocked. So, Taba Castle?"

"No, this is Fort Nuweiba, another ruin in the same region." Crystal spun the wheel on her mouse, zooming in on the weathered ramparts. "Best I can tell, everything looks completely normal. Taba Castle, on the other hand, is still nowhere to be seen."

Angelique's brow furrowed. Whatever was going on in the desert seemed to be confined to that one ruin. She wished she knew what made that place so special, but other than its relatively minor role in the Crusades, neither she nor Crystal had found anything of note.

"Did you need anything in particular, boss?" Crystal asked, snapping her out of her thoughts.

"Yes. Anatoly encountered a group of killers in Cairo and they were unaffected by his magic."

Crystal sucked in a breath. "That's... not great."

"No." Angelique handed her the copy of the picture he sent. "They all had daggers like this one. I need you to dig up everything you can find on them. At a glance I can't see anything especially remarkable about it."

Crystal peered closer at the photo. "I'll do my best, but it would help to have the actual dagger to analyze."

"Once Daisuke finds a secure base of operations, I'll have him bring it here. For now, just learn what you can."

"Okay, boss. Is this a super-secret thing or can I consult with experts?"

"As long as you're circumspect about the source of the

image, feel free to ask around. We're in no position to turn down any help we might get. Good luck." Angelique left Crystal to her work and walked out of the computer lab.

A few strides down the hall brought her to Donny's magical research lab. She always hated bothering him given how stressful he found talking with people, but this was too important.

Angelique knocked and waited a moment.

No response.

She knocked again, harder. "Donny? It's urgent. You don't have to open the door, but we need to talk."

Silence stretched for a long moment before a hesitant, muffled voice said, "What do you need?"

With Donny, short was best so she got right to the point. "Anatoly encountered magic-resistant assassins. Anything you can dig up about spells or items that make someone immune to magic would be helpful."

"Any additional parameters?"

"The effect is personal with a range of maybe a foot from the body. Beyond that I have no idea."

"No, that's helpful. I can leave out magic dead zones in my search. I'll send you a message if I find anything." His retreating footsteps made it clear Donny had said all he planned to.

And that was fine. Less stress meant faster results.

Having done all she could down here, Angelique made her way back to her office. Time to give Helena and Jinx the bad news that their break had been canceled.

Helena gazed out the jet's window at the blue expanse of the Mediterranean, a satisfied smile playing across her lips. Leaving Odessa came as a relief. They'd accomplished a lot, but it would be good to get home and sleep in her own bed.

In the seat across from her, Jinx slouched, eyes half closed, head resting on the cabin wall. Despite Helena's worries when they started out, their partnership had worked out well. She still didn't know what they were going to do about their mutual feelings for Daisuke. Especially since Helena didn't know what to do about her own mixed-up feelings. Figuring out where Jinx fit into the mix gave her a headache.

"Sergeant Rostolov looked like he might cry from relief when we told him it was over," Jinx said.

"Are you surprised?" Helena asked. "For a regular cop, there are few things more difficult to deal with than magic. He held it together pretty well all things considered. I just hope Dagon's hellpriests don't decide to get aggressive. Odessa deserves a break."

"They aren't the only ones," Jinx said.

Helena couldn't argue. Despite Daisuke doing the bulk of the heavy lifting at the end, it had been a long couple of days.

The view shifted as the plane banked. Helena frowned, but before she could say anything the pilot's voice spoke over the intercom. "We've been ordered to divert to Istanbul."

Jinx sat up straight and they exchanged a look.

"Istanbul? Isn't that where Daisuke was headed?" Jinx asked. "You don't think he's in trouble already?"

Helena pursed her lips, turning the possibilities over in her mind. "I can't see how. He left Zurich sometime today. Even for him, finding trouble this fast is unlikely."

Helena's phone rang and she pulled it out of her pocket. The boss's number was on the screen. She hit speaker so Jinx could listen. "What's happening, boss? Is Daisuke alright?"

"Yes, he's fine, but there's been a change of plans. I had to send Daisuke to Cairo so he could assist Anatoly. The situation there is deteriorating quickly. Dealing with the death glider falls to you two. I know you need a break, but it's going to have to wait."

That was pretty vague. Either she didn't know more or she didn't want to risk the flight crew overhearing how bad the situation had grown. Helena couldn't decide which one worried her more.

"We understand," Helena said. "Don't worry, we'll take care of it."

"I knew I could count on you two. You'll be meeting Captain Ali of the Istanbul Security Services at a cafe called the Coffee Cup. His superiors aren't exactly thrilled about needing outside help. When two women show up, well, just tread carefully. Ali's my only contact in Istanbul and I'd prefer not to do anything that might burn him."

"Understood, boss. We'll be on our best behavior. Once we finish with the death glider are we going to Zurich or Cairo?" Helena wasn't sure which answer she was hoping for. Exhaustion nearly overwhelmed her worry about Daisuke.

"Not sure yet. Hopefully Zurich, but circumstances on the ground will determine that. Contact me when you're finished." The line went dead and Helena pocketed her phone.

"Well," Jinx said. "So much for our break. What sort of craziness do you think we'll find in Istanbul?"

"Heaven may know, but I certainly don't." Helena

yawned. “Whatever we run into, I hope it isn’t as bad as Odessa.”

“I second that,” Jinx said. “Sounds like Daisuke’s going to be too busy to bail us out if we get in deep this time.”

Helena couldn’t argue. As much as she disliked relying on anyone, knowing they could call him in should the worst happen soothed her nerves in a way nothing else could.

This time, they’d have to sort it all out themselves.

CHAPTER FOUR

Daisuke studied the run-down facade of Lilly's Frocks, his gaze shifting between the cracked windows and peeling paint. This area might be nicer than the Cairo slums, but not by much. On the plus side, it seemed Lilly had a thriving business. While he and Anatoly had been watching, half a dozen customers came and went.

"Are you sure this is it?" Anatoly asked. "I can't imagine someone so careful wanting to live in such a busy place."

"On the contrary. With so many people coming and going it would be simple for her clients to blend into the crowd. That said, I have no interest in going through the front door. Let's check for a back way in."

The two men circled the building, passing through an empty alley and sending a nervous cat running. A rickety metal staircase clung to the rear wall. It led to the second-floor apartment landing. Daisuke sensed no one around, which worked out perfectly for them.

"Take a peek inside," Daisuke said. "I'll keep watch."

Anatoly closed his eyes and the ether stirred.

While he did his thing, Daisuke said, "Ruq, get up on the roof and keep an eye out. I'd prefer not to have anyone show up unannounced."

"You'll hear them coming as soon as they put a toe on that ladder." There was a slight pressure on his shoulder when Ruq pushed off.

No one showed the least interest in them and after a long minute Anatoly said, "Cluttered as hell, but no knife-wielding killers. Should be okay to go in."

They crossed the street then climbed the steps, which creaked and shuddered every bit as loudly as he'd feared. On the landing Daisuke twisted the cheap-looking doorknob. Locked, of course.

Well, it would take more than a locked door to stop a wizard. Daisuke shaped an ethereal key and popped the lock. He slipped inside the cramped apartment with Anatoly a step behind. The curtains, pulled so tight only a sliver of light entered from the edges, left them in the dark. He flicked the light switch and grimaced at the chaos.

Stacks of books and papers covered the dining room table. The sour scent of old beer mixed with dust and mildew. Somewhere, water dripped in irregular beats. Finding anything useful in this disaster would take a miracle.

Looks a bit like our kitchen table.

Daisuke ignored Ruq's sarcasm, sighed, relocked the door, and shrugged off his jacket. "You take the bedroom, I'll start in here."

Anatoly nodded. "Thank you for your consideration."

Daisuke grinned. "You're the one who got stabbed. Seemed the least I could do."

Anatoly worked his way around the loaded table and stepped through the room's only door.

Daisuke wished him a silent good luck and got to work sorting his own mess. A collection of recent newspapers sat on top. He paged through them but found nothing highlighted or circled. Next came a pile of opposition research on some member of parliament he'd never heard of.

For some reason he'd imagined this chick specialized in magical information. Why he'd thought that he had no idea. He didn't sense so much as a spark of magic in this place. No way was she a wizard.

"Daisuke," Anatoly called from the bedroom. "I found something."

Thank heaven for small favors. Daisuke marched over to the bedroom door. Anatoly stood by the far wall, an open section of it revealing a hidden niche.

"Well, well, what have we here?" Daisuke moved to join Anatoly beside the niche.

Inside, he found stacks of paper covered in neatly typed, double-spaced script; an old, leather-bound journal; and last but not least, a dagger, twin to the one Anatoly took from the guy who stabbed him.

"Now we can each have one." Daisuke held up the dagger. It had decent heft and a keen-looking edge, but nothing else about it struck him as remarkable.

"I think I can guess why they killed her," Anatoly said.

"No kidding. We need to read all her notes, but not here." Daisuke took out his wallet and removed a certain metal card. He sent a stream of ether into it then tossed it on the broker's bed. As soon as it hit, the card transformed into his trunk. "I'll load this stuff up. Want to check the kitchen?"

"I don't mind, but do you think there'll be anything there?"

"Probably not, but better safe than sorry. You can throw your dagger in here as well if you want."

"Thanks. I was getting tired of hanging on to it." Anatoly tossed the dagger on top of Daisuke's spare t-shirt and went toward the kitchen. If he found anything, it would be a surprise, but hardly the biggest Daisuke had ever encountered.

It didn't take long to load everything up. Daisuke wanted to quickly page through the journal before tossing it in but Ruq's telepathic voice popped into his head, stopping him before he could crack the cover.

Company coming toward the outside steps. If the cheap suits and pistols are any indication, they're cops.

Daisuke heard the squeak a moment later and grimaced. He hadn't expected the cops to get involved until they had put more distance between themselves and this dump. Talk about rotten luck.

He tossed the journal in and returned his trunk to card form. That done, he hurried to the kitchen. "We have to go. Cops incoming."

"Go where?" Anatoly asked. "I didn't find another exit."

Daisuke strengthened himself with a spell. "The shadow paths."

Anatoly opened his mouth to argue but the steps were getting closer by the second.

"No other options. Hang on." Before he could say anything else, Daisuke lifted the other man on his shoulder, careful not to touch his wound, and stepped into a shadow.

A heartbeat later they emerged in an alley across the

street from the rear exit. Daisuke wrapped them both in invisibility and set Anatoly on his feet.

"That was unpleasant," Anatoly said. "Do you often travel in such fashion?"

"Yes. I can be anywhere in the world in a few seconds. It's very convenient."

Anatoly grunted and assumed control of his share of the invisibility spell.

Daisuke put his companion out of his mind and focused on the cops. He listened through his connection to Ruq. They hammered on the door as if expecting the dead woman to answer.

"Cairo PD! Open up!" one of them said, loud enough that he had no trouble hearing without using Ruq's ears.

"Do they not know she's dead after all?" Anatoly asked.

Daisuke had no idea and assumed it was a rhetorical question in any case.

The silence dragged on and the cops exchanged glances. The shorter one pulled a pick gun from his pocket and set to work on the lock. In seconds, the door swung open. Hands on their sidearms, they ducked inside.

"You think someone in the slums saw us and called it in?" Anatoly asked.

Daisuke frowned. "I doubt anyone in the slums is keen to chat with the cops. And even if they did, how would they know where to find her apartment? She had no ID on her. I think the cops are looking for us."

"We were set up?" Anatoly's eyes narrowed and Daisuke could see a hint of the Russian's aggressive side.

"I'm not sure that's the right word, but if we end up in a cell for however long it takes them to figure out we didn't kill the broker, it will certainly slow us down. Five'll get you ten your buddies with the daggers called them, anonymously, I'm sure."

Anatoly let out a little growl. "I'll reach out to the Circle's contact in the department and see what she knows."

"Good idea." Daisuke never took his gaze off the apartment door. He didn't know what the cops thought they might find up there, but if they didn't fancy political rumormongering litter, they were going to end up disappointed.

Ten minutes passed before the door swung open and the two cops stalked out, their faces twisted in frustration. The sight pleased Daisuke no end. They'd come up empty-handed, exactly as he expected.

The older one yanked a radio from his belt. "Send up the observation units, now!"

Beside him, Anatoly shifted, wincing as the movement pulled at his wound. "Time to go?"

"Almost. I want to see where they position the stakeout. Hopefully we won't have to come back, but if we do, I want to know what to expect." Daisuke's gaze shifted to his companion. "How's the side?"

"Still sore but no longer bleeding. After food and sleep I'll give it a second application of healing magic. That should finish the repairs."

The squeak of tires hitting the curb dragged his attention back to the apartment. Two unmarked cars had parked on the curb and the older cop had his head stuck in the front driver-side window of the lead car. Daisuke couldn't hear what they were saying but he could imagine.

When the conversation ended, one of the cars pulled around to the front. Daisuke watched it through Ruq's eyes. They parked where they would have a good view of the shop's front door. The second car parked in the back, facing away from the building. Clever; they could watch in the rearview mirror while looking disinterested.

Daisuke had seen enough. “I assume you’ve got a hotel.”

“Of course. Though given the amount of time I’ve been spending in Cairo, I should’ve rented an apartment. It would’ve been cheaper.”

Daisuke grinned. “Not like it’s your money. This is what expense accounts are for. Let’s get out of here. We’ve got reading to do.”

CHAPTER FIVE

The door of the Coffee Cup Cafe had been carved with, uncreatively enough, a steaming mug. And while the design might not have been the most original, whoever did the work had an eye for detail. The mug, saucer, and wisps of steam were all perfectly done. Helena shoved the distracting thought aside. They had work to do and she didn't have time to waste taking in the scenery.

A group of pedestrians ambled past on the bustling Istanbul sidewalk, paying no mind to two women lingering outside the quaint establishment.

"How do you want to handle this?" Jinx asked. "The boss made it sound like we shouldn't expect a warm welcome."

"Ali should be okay. If he's a Circle contact he must know we have as many women in the group as men. He deals with the boss all the time. I suspect the real problem is his superiors. Some men have fragile egos and you don't rise far in politics without an ego. In this part of the world, it's also a cultural thing." Helena shrugged. "With any luck we can avoid the higher-ups and just deal with Ali. I'll handle the talking. You keep an eye out for any signs of trouble, okay?"

"Sure, I can do that."

Right, no more delays. Helena pushed the door open and the little bell over the door jingled. The rich aroma of roasted coffee beans wafted over them, swirling with notes of cardamom and clove. Boisterous chatter in Turkish and Arabic filled the space, punctuated by the clinking of cups on saucers and the hiss of milk steamers. Amber lighting glowed from mosaic pendant lamps, which cast intricate patterns on the scarlet cushions of the booths. Seemed like too nice a spot for a meeting about demons.

Helena scanned the room, her gaze passing over patrons hunched over chessboards and a group of men gesticulating as they argued. No sign of Captain Ali. The boss had been kind of vague on the details beyond saying he'd be wearing a white suit. No one here fit even that minimal description.

A young waitress in a burgundy apron approached them with a bright smile. "Please, sit anywhere you'd like." Her English had only a slight accent.

"Actually, we're supposed to be meeting someone," Helena said. "Captain Ali should be expecting us."

The waitress's eyes lit up with recognition. "Ah, yes! The captain has reserved one of our private rooms for you. Right this way, please."

She beckoned them toward the back of the cafe. They wove through the tables, drawing passing glances, but nothing that triggered Helena's danger sense. So far, the cafe seemed like any other in Istanbul, a warm gathering place filled with boisterous locals fueled by strong coffee.

The waitress led them to the very back of the cafe, to a short hallway lined with four doors. She gestured at them.

"These are our private dining rooms, for parties or business meetings that require a bit more discretion. Captain Ali is waiting for you in the last one."

"Thank you very much." It seemed Ali was a better planner than Helena had feared.

The waitress rapped on the last door before cracking it open and poking her head inside. "Captain, the rest of your party has arrived."

A deep, melodious voice from inside said, "Ah, excellent. Please, send them in."

With a smile and a wave of her hand, the waitress ushered Helena and Jinx through the doorway. "Can I bring you anything to drink? Some coffee or tea perhaps?"

Helena shook her head. "No, thank you, we're fine for now."

"As you wish. There's a bell pull should you change your mind." The young woman dipped her chin and exited, closing the door softly behind her.

The small, simply appointed private room had plain, whitewashed walls and a round wooden table surrounded by four chairs. A single man, about the ugliest Helena had ever laid eyes on, occupied one of the chairs. The bronze skin of his face had deep pockmarks and a thick black unibrow ran over both eyes. His dark hair had nearly vanished, yet he still made a vain attempt at a combover. He stood as they entered. He wore a white linen suit cut to fit his muscular frame.

A grin spread across his face as his gaze landed on Helena and Jinx. "My, my. When I was told I'd be meeting with two lady wizards I never imagined anyone so beautiful."

He gave an exaggerated waggle of his bushy unibrow. Helena barely suppressed a shudder. They had no other contacts and as long as he tried nothing other than leering, she'd let him off the hook. Heaven knew she'd encountered more than her fair share of such men over the years.

"Please, sit." He motioned to the chairs in front of him.

Helena settled in beside Jinx and crossed her arms. "Captain Ali, pleasure to meet you. I'm Helena, this is my partner Jinx. What can you tell us about the Death Glider?"

Ali sighed. "Yes, best we get right to it. Some of my superiors are less than enthusiastic about having to rely on outside help. Best for all of us if we deal with the demon as quickly as possible and get you ladies on your way. The smugglers have been using the demon to spy on our patrol ships, relaying their positions, and allowing the criminals to evade capture."

"That doesn't sound too bad," Helena said.

He shook his head and made a face. "It gets worse. They've also unleashed it against their rivals. Nearly a dozen ships destroyed and their crews slaughtered."

"Have they only attacked criminals?" Helena asked.

"How I wish. Three civilian crafts have been among the victims. The last one belonged to a cousin of the security chief." Ali lowered his voice as if they weren't alone in the room. "That's when he decided to allow the Circle to come in and deal with the thing."

"Nothing like having your hand forced to put you in a bad mood."

"Yes," Ali said. "But mark my words, once they've wiped out the competition, they'll come for the coast guard next. Then they'll control the shipping lanes. It would be a catastrophe!"

Helena had trouble imagining that the government lacked a wizard capable of dealing with such a low tier demon, but that wasn't her problem. Best to focus on the task at hand.

"I assume you have a plan for getting us within striking distance?" Helena said. "Something the damn thing won't see from fifty miles away."

The captain smiled, but there was no humor in it. "Indeed, we have a scheme in mind. Although I must confess, you may not be crazy about it."

Helena didn't like the sound of that in the least. "Why don't you lay it out for us and we'll decide just how much we dislike it."

He nodded and took a deep breath as if steeling himself. "Basically, we made a deal with a group of captured smugglers. You join their crew while they serve as bait to lure the demon in. If the mission is successful, they get a full pardon. The offer has made them highly motivated."

"I'll bet," Helena said. "Still, it's not the worst plan I've ever heard. Jinx and I can handle some scruffy smugglers should they get ideas, and bringing the demon to us is a much better idea than trying to hunt down something specialized in spotting enemies coming."

Ali slumped in comical relief. "Then you agree?"

"We do. How soon can we get started?"

"First light tomorrow. I've arranged a hotel for you and I'll pick you up myself in the morning." Ali held out a sweaty hand. "We are all most grateful for your help in this matter."

Helena gave his moist palm a quick shake. She'd rather fight the demon than have to do that again.

CHAPTER SIX

Daisuke had to admit Anatoly had chosen the perfect hotel. It had a golden sphinx over the revolving door, its paws supporting a red awning. Someone had painted the whole thing to look like they'd built it from the same stone as the pyramids. The place hit every Egyptian stereotype and added a few new ones for good measure. Nobody in a million years would think to look here for two wizards trying to keep a low profile.

"This place is certainly something," Daisuke said as they pushed through the revolving door. "Hopefully they have a spare room."

The interior decorations resembled a museum display. Fake artifacts on pedestals sat scattered around here and there under lights that made the plastic even more obvious. If they didn't have so much to do he would've been tempted to check out the restaurant, but that would have to keep for now.

"Despite its appearance," Anatoly said. "The rates are

quite reasonable and the food tasty. I'm on the fifth floor, room six. Try to get something adjoining."

They went to the front desk where a severe woman dressed like a painting of Nefertiti glowered at them. Daisuke couldn't even get upset with her attitude. If he'd had to work here, he would've been pissed too.

A brief conversation secured him the room across from Anatoly's. Not quite as good as adjoining, but it would suffice. Leaving the queen to survey her realm, they headed for the elevators.

As soon as the doors closed, Ruq said, "I love this place. If there was a demon lord of bad taste, this would be his temple. Do you think they have baklava?"

"Beats me," Daisuke said. "We'll ask room service when we're finished working."

The elevator doors slid open and Daisuke and Anatoly stepped out onto the worn red carpet. Anatoly led the way down the hallway, fishing a key card from his pocket. He swiped it and pushed open the door.

The hotel room appeared every bit as remarkable as everything else about the hotel. Hieroglyphics decorated the walls and the rather lumpy-looking bed resembled a sarcophagus. A quick glance through the bathroom door confirmed the sink faucet looked like a cobra.

"I hope the boss sends Helena and Jinx to join us," Daisuke said. "They've got to see this place."

Anatoly grunted and pulled out his phone. "I'll check in with our contact at the police department."

"Good idea." Daisuke summoned his trunk on the floor and popped it open. "I'll see if I can make sense of this chaos."

"More reading," Ruq said. "Fantastic."

"And this time you're helping. We just need to get it organized for now."

He sat on the floor and pulled all the papers out, followed by the journal and daggers which he set to one side. Daisuke shoved half the pile of papers toward Ruq, who let out a dramatic sigh.

Thankfully the imp's complaints ended there. Not that all the complaints in the world would've changed what they needed to do.

He grabbed the first page and scanned it. The heading mentioned the Order of the Veiled Cross, whatever that was. The next three papers mentioned the order as well and the little he read indicated they were Crusaders. Daisuke had heard of the Knights Templar and the Teutonic Order—they studied them in school—but he'd never heard of the Order of the Veiled Cross. They must not have accomplished much.

Why in the world would a Cairo information broker be interested in them?

The next paper moved to a more recent subject, a gentleman by the name of Mustafa Khalil. The article indicated Mr. Khalil had donated ten million Euros to the local museum, which named a wing after him.

Page after page went into one pile or the other. So far he'd found information on only Mustafa and the Veiled Cross. The latter's pile was a good deal thinner than the former's. The broker had built an extensive dossier on Mustafa, including photos, financial records, personal details—you name it and this chick had info on it. The why, on the other hand, eluded Daisuke.

Lost in thought, he almost didn't notice when Anatoly ended his call. "You were right, someone tipped off the police. They claimed they saw the murderer fleeing the scene. Can you guess the description they gave?"

"Yours?"

"Bingo."

"Just yours?"

Anatoly nodded.

"That's something. The killers must not've seen me. I should be free to move around without drawing attention."

"I, on the other hand, will be useless. My contact wants me to come in and clear everything up, but that could take days."

"Might be wise to wait until our business here is complete. And you won't be useless. With your scrying magic you can do almost as much from here as on the street." From Anatoly's glum expression Daisuke decided his effort at reassurance had fallen flat. Perhaps a change of subject. "Ever heard of a Mustafa Khalil?"

"Of course. He was the collector the Spirit Eaters killed when they stole the Elemental Orb."

"Well, Ahmed's girlfriend knew everything about the guy. I seriously doubt that was a coincidence."

Anatoly frowned. "You think Ahmed had her investigate Mustafa before stealing the orb?"

"Looks like it. Maybe that's how they met."

"Perhaps. And now they're both as dead as Mustafa."

Daisuke rubbed his temples. "How about the Order of the Veiled Cross? They were a bunch of Crusaders."

Anatoly shook his head. "That's a new one to me."

"Me too. Maybe the journal will shed some light on all this."

He was about to reach for it when his phone rang. "Yeah, boss?"

"Daisuke, have you found a secure base of operations?"

"You could call it that. Why?"

"I need you to bring the dagger Anatoly took from his attacker here so Crystal can investigate it fully. She can only do so much with a picture."

"Sure, not a problem. We've made a bit of progress on this end so I'll give you a full report when I get there. Just a sec."

He hung up and turned to Anatoly. "I have to run home. You look all in. This stuff will keep until I get back. Why don't you take a nap?"

"I like that plan. It has been a bit of a day."

That was one way to put it. Daisuke grabbed the new dagger they found in the information broker's apartment and stood. The shadows separating the bathroom from the rest of the space were the deepest so he used them. A moment later he entered the shadow paths and headed for Zurich.

He emerged from the teleportation chamber at the same time the boss stepped out of her office. He held out the dagger. "Here you go, one dagger as ordered."

She took it and gave the weapon a once-over. Daisuke hadn't found anything when he checked it and he doubted she would either. It was just a sharp dagger, nothing at all special about it.

"Not so much as a spark of magic," she said at last. "How's Anatoly?"

"No longer bleeding. He's going to rest. I've got a pile of reading waiting for me when I get back. Want to hear what we've learned so far?"

"Let's walk and talk. Crystal is eager to get her hands on this."

"Really? It doesn't have a screen or batteries."

The boss's lips quirked up a fraction. "True, but she does enjoy solving mysteries. Donny's looking into the anti-magic thing as well."

They set out for the basement and he said, "I'd certainly like some answers before I have to fight them, pistol or not. Anyway, we found some intel hidden in a secret compartment in the dead woman's apartment. Hopefully some of it has her name since I'm getting tired of thinking of her by her job title."

When he'd finished filling her in they'd reached the bottom of the steps. The boss knocked on Crystal's door and said, "You think the killers are related to the Veiled Cross?"

"Good a guess as any, but why modern-day killers would have anything to do with a thousand-year-old group of Crusaders is beyond me. Hopefully I'll learn more after I finish reading the papers. You want me to go back or stick around?"

"Go back. I don't like the idea of Anatoly being alone, especially with the police looking for him. Keep me posted."

"Will do, boss. Before I go, how are Helena and Jinx doing? I feel kind of bad they had to step in for me."

"They made contact with Ali, but I haven't gotten another update. Don't be too hard on yourself. You can't be in more than one place and Cairo took priority."

"Thanks, boss. See you later." He headed back up the steps. It was time to get down to reading.

As Daisuke's footsteps receded, Angelique put him out of her mind and turned toward the door to Crystal's computer room. He seemed to have things under control at the moment, so the best thing she could do was get him more information about the threats he faced.

She knocked and pushed the door open. For the first time in maybe ever, Crystal sat facing her, an eager smile splitting her face. The whole scene looked so unnatural, a moment of worry hit her. Angelique shook it off a second later. Crystal looked excited, not upset.

Before Angelique could speak, Crystal said, "I think I've found the origin of that dagger."

Angelique stopped beside her desk. "Let me guess, the Order of the Veiled Cross?"

Crystal's face fell. "How did you know?"

"Daisuke discovered some clues." Angelique held out the dagger. "Here you go."

Crystal reached for it. "Excellent. Now I can confirm if it really is a Veiled Cross dagger. If it is, there should be a symbol stamped on the tang. An inverted sword on a shield. Now I just need to find a grinder."

"Let me see." Angelique took the dagger back and summoned ether into the pad of her thumb. Next she touched her glowing thumb to the peened metal, disintegrating it a bit at a time until the pommel loosened.

She handed the dagger back to Crystal. "You do the honors."

Crystal wiggled the pommel off then slid the hilt off the tang. And there it was. "The inverted sword and shield, just like the museum piece I found online. It's definitely from the Order of the Veiled Cross. What I don't get is how those killers got their hands on it. I mean, relics from the Order are crazy rare. There are only half a dozen daggers on display in the whole world, at least that I could find. The odds of these people having four of them seems... low."

"Indeed, and of greater interest is why they're using them in the first place. A simple tactical knife would be every bit as deadly and easily found in a hardware store. What else have you learned about them?"

Crystal shook her head, looking deflated. "Not a whole lot yet, but I just got started. I'll find more."

Angelique patted her shoulder. "I don't doubt that for a moment. Keep up the good work."

She left the computer room and retreated to her office. They'd learned a few things, but so much remained to be done and the killers were still out there.

CHAPTER SEVEN

Daisuke returned to Anatoly's hotel room via the same shadow he used to leave. The older man lay sprawled on the bed, sound asleep. Poor guy had been through the wringer. If anyone deserved a good night's sleep, he did. Not wanting to risk waking him, Daisuke cast a silence spell, gathered the papers and journal into his trunk, and slipped into the hallway.

Two strides brought him to his door and Ruq used his key card to unlock it. A magical nudge pushed the door open and he entered.

Ruq flipped on the light then flew over to the nightstand and pulled the drawer open. "Aha!" The imp waved a room service menu. "They have baklava. Want me to order?"

"Sure, go nuts." Daisuke put his trunk at the base of the bed and piled the papers on top. Finally he sank into the room's sole armchair with the leather-bound journal. It looked like the most interesting bit and he wanted to dive into it first.

Ignoring Ruq's cackling as he dialed, Daisuke flipped the journal open to the first page.

May 19th, 1291, Penned by Sir Hugh de Vandon:

The Mamluks have taken Acre. Our brave soldiers fought well, but, alas, their numbers overwhelmed us. Barely two score of the order escaped the carnage, fleeing south for Taba Castle. Sir Raymond commands our ragged band. He is confident we can reach the castle ahead of the Mamluk dogs. I pray to Branik his faith is not misplaced.

Daisuke stopped reading, mulling the knight's ominous words. The name Taba Castle didn't ring any bells, but that meant nothing given his general disinterest in the Crusades as a whole. He got his phone out and pulled up the notes app to jot down items for further research. That done, he moved on to the next entry.

The date jumped forward to May 23rd. Sir Hugh's script grew more frantic, the lines slanting and jagged across the page.

. . .

The Mamluks are relentless in their pursuit. Each dawn when we rise to press on, their dust clouds appear on the horizon behind us. They are like jackals, loping after wounded prey, waiting for us to falter.

Our men and mounts grow weary. I fear we cannot maintain this grueling pace much longer. But Sir Raymond rallies the men, swears that if we reach Taba, the castle's defenses will keep us safe. His conviction lends strength to us all. We must keep faith.

May 30th.

Taba Castle, at last! Our desperate flight is over. As the castle's pale ramparts rose from the shimmering desert sands, I nearly wept with relief.

We thundered through the gates mere minutes ahead of the Mamluks. Men and beasts alike collapsed in the courtyard, chests heaving, pushed beyond all endurance.

The portcullis crashed down. From the keep strode our venerable leader, High Warden Sir Thomas de Chalons. He praised our resilience and clasped Raymond's shoulder as our commander struggled to stand and report.

"Acre has fallen," Raymond gasped out. "We are all that remain of our order beyond these walls. The Mamluks follow behind us, hungry for our blood. They will lay siege soon."

"Let them come!" Sir Thomas boomed. "We have long prepared for this day. The weapon will scour them from the field like chaff before the wind. Take heart and rest now. We must be ready when the enemy arrives."

Raymond sagged with relief at this promise. In Sir Thomas we trusted fully for he had never led us astray. Surely our prayers are answered.

Daisuke frowned, trying to imagine what sort of weapon they might've had back then capable of turning such an overwhelming tide. He flipped the page, eager to find out.

June 1st.

The Mamluks arrived with the dawn, rank upon rank of turbaned soldiers ringing Taba Castle. Siege towers loomed, trebuchets creaked, and war drums pounded as the army prepared its assault.

Sir Raymond gripped the rampart with such force I feared he might crack the stone beneath his gauntlets. Beside him, Sir Thomas watched the preparations with an unreadable expression. He clutched a strange, wrapped bundle about half the size of a newborn. The high warden has shared no details of this weapon, at least not in my hearing.

"Crusaders!" The cry rang out, echoing off the walls. A richly armored Mamluk rode forward, reining in his white stallion. "I am Turan al-Khalil! Surrender now and you may depart in peace! Resist, and your bones shall bleach beneath the sun! Choose swiftly!"

Daisuke jerked upright. Al-Khalil. That was the dead businessman's name. Was he a descendent of this commander or was it a coincidence? He made a note to investigate later.

Refocusing on the faded pages, he read on, pulse quickening. Things were about to get good.

Sir Thomas stepped forward, inclining his head to the Mamluk. Then he unwrapped the bundle with deliberate motions.

Bronze gleamed in the harsh Egyptian sun. The ancient urn was unlike any of the other vile artifacts the order had collected over the centuries. It had a shallow impression at the top graven with an occult symbol. As the high warden placed a disk in the impression and raised the urn overhead, the top vanished and darkness streamed from its mouth, billowing into an all-consuming wave. He shouted an order in a language I had never heard before.

Screams mingled with inhuman roars. The dying shrieks of men and horses will haunt my dreams until Branik claims my soul. Raymond stumbled back, hand fumbling for his sword. It was all I could do not to faint. And then the darkness vanished, sucked back into the urn as swiftly as it had appeared.

Carnage greeted my eyes. The once-mighty army lay strewn in pieces across the sands, broken bodies and shattered siege machines destroyed by some unspeakable force. Despite the darkness's vile nature, not a soul within the castle had been harmed.

"It is done." Sir Thomas pocketed the disk and rewrapped the urn with shaking hands, his face ashen and wan. The high warden

staggered off, followed by the stares of the knights lining the battlements. Each gaze held the same bafflement I felt. What evil had been unleashed here and would our souls survive it?

Daisuke closed the journal, a chill racing up his spine. A demon prison, the description fit perfectly. Sounded like the high warden had a rough time with the corruption; no doubt lacking access to the Staff of Law didn't help.

Which of the seventy-two had they summoned? There was no description of the demon or the rune, so he didn't even know how to ask the boss to look it up.

A knock on the door interrupted his dark thoughts. Right, room service. Daisuke desperately needed something sweet. Since Ruq had ordered, he felt confident he'd have plenty to choose from.

He pulled the door open and found a young man waiting with a laden cart. "Your order, sir."

"Thanks." Daisuke gave him a five-Euro tip and brought the cart in. The sweet smells from the covered plates made his mouth water.

They dug into the desserts, including the much anticipated baklava. Halfway through the meal Daisuke said, "The Crusaders got their hands on one of Solomon's prisons. From the sounds of it, they were a sort of OG version of the Circle, collecting corrupt artifacts for safekeeping."

"Or just for keeping," Ruq said around a mouthful of cookie.

"Maybe. Their base was a place called Taba Castle. Bet we could find all sorts of interesting things there. At a minimum we need to collect the prison and add the seal to the Staff of Law."

"Where is it?" Ruq asked.

"Damn good question. With any luck the rest of the papers will have the answer."

Daisuke sighed and patted his stomach. He was pretty sure Ruq had ordered every dessert the hotel offered, and he found them all equally delicious. His familiar busied himself with licking the last of the honey off the baklava platter with a tongue nearly as long as his body. Luckily, Helena wasn't here to see him. Ruq's table manners disgusted her.

"She's too sensitive," Ruq said. "Given the crap we deal with on a regular basis my table manners are nothing."

Daisuke couldn't argue with that and he'd long since gotten to the point where nothing Ruq did bothered him. Putting questions of etiquette out of his mind, he settled back in his chair to finish the journal. Somehow Daisuke doubted it would have a happy ending.

He picked up where he left off, June 2nd.

Sir Thomas hasn't slept since he summoned the unholy darkness. He has also refused to return the artifact to the castle vault. Those who have seen him claim he carries the bronze urn with him always, clutching it like a beloved child to his breast.

Rumors swirl through our ranks. Has the darkness taken hold of him? Is our leader now a thrall to the evil we swore to defeat?

None of us can answer the question and that haunts me. If the high warden can fall to corruption, what hope is there for the rest of us?

Daisuke's brow furrowed. Sounded like the demon had gotten its hooks into Sir Thomas. That's why untrained people shouldn't try to use the seals to command Solomon's demons. How did the saying go, when you looked into the darkness you had to be careful since the darkness looked back into you? Something like that. If you didn't take precautions, demons would have an easy time messing with your head.

He flipped to the next entry, dated June 5th. The script was erratic, the lines jagged and uneven, as if penned by a trembling hand. Daisuke squinted, straining to decipher the frantic text. Clearly things had not improved for the unfortunate Sir Hugh.

Sir Thomas summoned the knights to the great hall, his visage gaunt and eyes alight with a feverish intensity. His voice rang out, declaring a new mission for our order.

"We shall harness the power of the artifacts we've amassed over centuries and use them to conquer these fractured lands! Under my enlightened rule, order shall prevail, and the petty squabbles of men will be silenced!"

I couldn't believe what I was hearing. Sir Thomas's words flew in the face of Branik's teachings and our order's founding principles. Silence met the announcement, confirming to me that my brothers were as horrified as I.

Seeing our lack of reaction, Sir Thomas stalked off muttering to the bronze urn as if the darkness inside could hear him. When he'd gone, the knights began speaking amongst themselves. None of us know what to do about this strange turn, but I have no doubt that we need to figure something out quickly lest the darkness consume us all.

Well, that ended up about how Daisuke had expected. Sir Thomas clearly fell under the demon's sway. Likely he didn't fully seal the urn after he let the demon out.

It was getting late but Daisuke read on. He had to see what happened next.

June 6th.

Sir Raymond gathered us in the courtyard, his face a mask of grim determination. "Sir Thomas has fallen," he declared, his voice heavy with sorrow. "We must act swiftly to bring him back to the light. And should we fail, the castle must be sealed away for all time."

He turned to the four most senior knights, men who had served with Sir Thomas since before I was born. "Will you go to him one last time? Reason with him. If your words can't bring him back to the light, I know not whose might."

The elder knights, their hair streaked with gray and their hard blue eyes surrounded by wrinkles and sunken into their faces as if driven there by decades under the sun, nodded. Their determination heartened us all. Surely these good men would not fail.

But fail they did. When, an hour later, they emerged from the keep, our hearts sank. They were changed, twisted, their eyes glowing with an unholy crimson light. They marched toward us at a dull, monotonous pace, all signs of who they once were missing.

"I will hold them here!" Sir Raymond said. "Seal the castle! We must bind this evil, at any cost."

I was loathe to leave my commander behind, but there was no question of what had to be done. I took a step to leave, but Sir Raymond grabbed my shoulder.

"Sir?"

"It will fall to you, my good Hugh, to rebuild the order. You and the other survivors must ensure no one can ever set free the evil we bind here."

He pushed me toward the castle gate and drew on Branik's holy might. White light shone around him and he charged the abominations that used to be our brothers.

I would weep for my friend, but not now. I joined the other knights in a mad dash for the gate. Once we were outside, the five wisest and bravest knights moved to surround the castle, their faces set with grim acceptance. They would anchor the barrier, though it cost their lives. Power grew until a dome of pure divine energy surrounded the castle.

Of the five knights, no sign remained. The magic had fully consumed them.

Daisuke turned to the final entry.

June 13th.

We have returned to Cairo, mere shadows of our former selves. Our armor and tabards, once proud symbols of our order, now lie abandoned. Only our daggers remain, a last vestige of our identity.

The weight of my task bears heavily upon me. Sir Raymond's final orders echo in my mind. "Rebuild the order," he said, "and protect the castle. Keep its evil hidden and forever contained."

But how? We are broken, lost. I am broken. All I ever knew has been consumed by darkness. I know I am not wise or clever. Yet, I must persevere. For the sake of all that is good, we must not falter.

Daisuke closed the journal. Damn, that was one hell of a story. He still hadn't decided what it all meant, but the picture had cleared a bit.

He yawned. For now, he was beat. The rest of the papers would keep until tomorrow. He pushed the room service cart out into the hallway then went to Anatoly's door and conjured a ward which would keep anyone from troubling his exhausted partner.

It took only a moment to repeat the process at his own

door. That done, he cleaned up and settled on his ludicrous-looking sarcophagus bed. Tomorrow, he felt certain, would be another busy day.

CHAPTER EIGHT

Helena tapped her foot on the cracked sidewalk outside their hotel. Ali said he'd be here at first light to pick them up. Well, the sun was peeking over the tips of the minarets and domes of the Istanbul skyline and she saw no sign of him. If she'd known he planned to be late, Helena could've kept resting in her room rather than standing out here enjoying the dubious smells of the city, an unpleasant blend of salt water, damp stone, and urban grit. Though prettier than Odessa, Istanbul had nothing else going for it.

She glanced at Jinx and found the half-demon standing quietly, looking perfectly at ease. If the delay bothered her, she gave no sign. It really shouldn't be bothering Helena this much. Her concern for Daisuke was making her short tempered. Not at all the mindset you wanted before going out on a demon hunt.

A vendor wheeled his cart past, the enticing scent of roasting chestnuts and fresh simit following in his wake. Maybe a quick snack would improve her mood. The thought had barely formed when a black sedan turned the corner with Ali behind the wheel.

"Finally." She took a deep breath and commanded herself to stay calm. The Circle had no other contacts in Istanbul and she didn't want to do anything that might cause Ali to reconsider their relationship.

The car pulled to a stop in front of the hotel. Helena yanked open the passenger door and slid into the front seat. Jinx clambered into the back and clicked her seatbelt.

"You're late." Helena pulled the door shut with a touch more force than necessary.

Ali pulled away from the curb. "Some things have happened. The demon attacked a coast guard ship last night."

"That's an escalation. What happened?"

Ali shook his head. "We have no details. All hands were killed. What we do have are the ship's last known coordinates. That's where you will begin the search. I was waiting for confirmation before I left headquarters. Which is why I'm late."

As reasons went, Helena could hardly find fault with his. "How did your superiors react?"

Ali looked her way, his smile humorless. "Exactly as you'd expect; poorly. On the plus side, even those who spoke against your participation in this matter have come around. You now have the enthusiastic support of the entire security apparatus."

Just what she always wanted. At a minimum it should eliminate any issues going forward.

The conversation ebbed and they made the rest of the trip in silence. Helena stared out the window, watching the city zoom by. It looked quite different from Zurich and completely different from the little town where she grew up in Iceland. Her work with the Circle had certainly brought her to some interesting places.

The car jolted to a halt, snapping Helena from her thoughts. She took in the chaos of the docks. Cranes loomed overhead, shipping containers hung from heavy cables and were stacked like multicolored building blocks as far as the eye could see.

They got out of the car and Jinx said, "I'm getting a sense of déjà vu."

Helena's lips twitched into a faint smile. "Let's hope no giant octopi show up."

Ali led them down the dock, his steps quick, just short of a jog. Helena matched his pace, ignoring the creaking and groaning cranes. First he shows up late, now he's practically running. The attack must've left Ali in a state.

At the end of the docks, a small group of men stood clustered near a battered fishing trawler. Years at sea had left their faces hard and weathered. They were dressed in worn, stained clothes. One of them, a wiry man with a scar running from his temple to his jaw, stepped forward, his eyes narrowing as he caught sight of Ali.

"These are the wizards?" he asked. His voice had a rough and grating quality Helena liked not in the least.

Ali nodded and handed him a scrap of paper. "The target coordinates. That's where you'll start, Captain Demir. I doubt it's where you'll finish, but it's better than driving around at random."

Captain Demir took the paper and shoved it in his pocket. "When it's finished we get our pardons, yes?"

"Exactly as your lawyer explained. Good luck." Without further ado, Ali turned and hurried back toward his car.

The men were all staring at Helena and Jinx. She didn't like their expressions at all.

"Shall we get underway?" Helena asked.

"By all means." Demir gestured at the barely floating excuse for a ship behind him. "Welcome aboard. I hope you've got strong stomachs as it's likely to be a rough ride."

"It wouldn't be the first one I've taken." Helena instantly regretted her choice of wording.

"I'll bet." Demir leered at her as Helena passed. When she was close, he leaned in, his breath hot against her ear. "It gets lonely out at sea. If you want to join me in the captain's cabin later, you're more than welcome."

He reached out, aiming for her backside, but half an inch from making contact, a crackle of golden energy snapped out. Demir yelped and yanked his hand back. Snarling, he lunged at her.

Helena moved faster. Her hand shot out, grabbed him by the throat with magically enhanced strength, and squeezed. "Try to touch me again and you won't have to worry about the demon. I'll kill you myself."

The rest of the crew started to move to their captain's defense. They barely managed a step when clawed hands rose out of their own shadows and twisted around their bodies, locking them in place.

"Let's all try to get along." Jinx smiled a beautiful smile even as her eyes blazed blood red.

The captain's eyes widened, lust instantly replaced by fear. It seemed Jinx had gotten through to him. Good; she didn't know where they'd find a new group of smugglers.

Helena released Demir with a shove. "I see we understand each other. This mission will go far more smoothly if we keep it strictly business. Don't you think?"

Demir gave an eager nod. "It will be exactly as you say, Miss. In fact, you two are welcome to share my cabin and I'll bunk with the men. That might be more comfortable for everyone."

Helena smiled. "I appreciate your attitude, Captain Demir. Jinx and I will take you up on your generous offer."

She stepped onto the ship's deck and Jinx joined her a moment later. The rest of the crew, now free of their shadowy bindings, hastened to get on board and get them underway. Helena found a spot out of the way in the rear of the ship.

Jinx leaned in and said, "You sounded like Daisuke."

"I can do a reasonable tough-guy impression, but people can usually tell I don't mean it. If Daisuke had been here, the first mate would've gotten a quick promotion and the captain a burial at sea. Anyway, it was your magic that really convinced them."

"I've used that spell a few times over the centuries. The shadows' touch seems to make humans uncomfortable, which is useful if you want to make threats. Don't worry about sleeping. Last night was a sleep night for me so I'm good for a week. I can keep watch while you rest."

That came as a relief. She could ward the door without issue, but knowing she had Jinx on watch would make her feel better. When had she come to have so much trust in the half-demon? Helena didn't know exactly, but she did know without a doubt she could count on Jinx to watch her back.

On this trip, she felt certain, they'd have nothing to rely on but each other.

CHAPTER NINE

Daisuke rubbed his bleary eyes as he pored over the scattered papers strewn across his bed. The mountain of carbs he'd shared with Ruq this morning had filled him up, but now it was back to the grind. He dearly hoped to get through the pile this morning. Exactly what he'd have to do after that remained an open question. He had his own opinion on the matter, but he wasn't in charge.

Whatever, future Daisuke could sort out that problem. Right now he had reading to do. He reached for the first stack of papers, the smaller one detailing—and he used that word lightly—the Order of the Veiled Cross. He'd found little, so far at least, not already covered in Sir Hugh's journal.

According to the historical overview, the Veiled Cross was the smallest and least renowned of the old Crusader orders. Just another band of holy warriors off to save the unenlightened. They weren't even a quarter the size of the Templars.

Hello, what have we here? Someone had scrawled a note in the margin. The unknown writer somehow figured out the true purpose of the order: collecting corrupt artifacts under the cover of fighting a war. That confirmed the journal's account. Why the order had kept their real motives hidden, even from their fellow knightly orders, remained a mystery. Perhaps they feared some of the others wouldn't approve.

He glanced at his phone again. Still no word from Anatoly. Healing himself must have really taken a toll. Having nearly died on multiple occasions, Daisuke had nothing but sympathy for him.

Returning to his work, Daisuke grabbed another report, this one detailing the Veiled Cross's desert stronghold. Supposedly the Mamluks destroyed Taba Castle when they wiped out the order. This report directly contradicted the journal and he had a pretty good idea why.

Sir Hugh and his successors had altered the story and historians bought it. If his theory proved true, he couldn't help wondering what had prompted those two archeologists the boss mentioned to go looking for the place. Maybe they hoped to find something interesting in whatever rubble remained. Still, few places in the world held more dangers than the Sinai. No one with a brain went there on a whim. He added a note to investigate the archeologists further.

The more he learned, the more questions he ended up with. He hated that part of these investigations the most. Daisuke vastly preferred having a target to collect or bad guys to kill. So much simpler, at least when his family didn't feel the need to get involved.

After another hour of reading he'd finished one pile of papers. Now for the stack on Mustafa. The documents painted a portrait of a successful trader, philanthropic and well-respected. But Daisuke knew how deceiving appearances could be.

Near the bottom of the pile he found a newspaper clipping with the headline: Local Businessman Mustafa Khalil Acquires Ancient Crystal For One Million Euros. Below the headline a photo showed the Elemental Orb in the hands of a smiling Middle Eastern man.

Someone, the broker Daisuke assumed, had written in large letters, SHOW AHMED.

That all but confirmed she was working with the late leader of the Spirit Eaters. He made a note in his phone with the date of the article and that he should ask Anatoly when the Spirit Eaters killed Mustafa.

He finished his reading but found nothing else of interest. Time to check in and drop off his haul. Daisuke gathered the scattered papers into a neat stack and piled them carefully into his trunk before transforming it back into a metal card.

"Ruq! Let's go."

His familiar lay sprawled out on a pillow, half passed out from all the sweets he'd eaten this morning and the night before. It never ceased to amaze Daisuke how much he could fit in that little body.

Ruq groaned and flapped over to land on his shoulder. "I can't believe I'm going to say this, but I don't want anything sweet."

"Nothing like a little overindulgence. Can demons even get upset stomachs?"

"This one can."

Daisuke grinned and stepped into a shadow.

Seconds later, he emerged in the familiar darkness of the

teleportation chamber in the Circle's headquarters. He went out into the hall and walked down to the boss's office.

Before he could knock, she opened the door. "Is there a problem? I didn't expect you back this soon."

"Not a problem exactly. I finished my reading and figured I'd bring the intel we found back for you. I'm not an expert at this stuff. You're liable to find something I missed."

"Come in and sit down. You can give me the condensed version."

Daisuke settled in his usual chair and laid out all that he'd learned. "Looks like the Veiled Cross knights let loose one of Astaroth's demons. At least that's my guess based on the description and the fact that it created undead servants."

"That's... a lot. Let me check the Book of Wisdom." She grabbed the leather-bound book off the corner of her desk and flipped to Astaroth's section.

While she was searching, he got out his trunk and put all the papers along with the journal on the opposite side of her desk. They finished at about the same time.

"Here it is." She tapped a finger on the page. "Umbral Tide, a greater demon and the second strongest of Astaroth's nine. The description says it takes the form of disembodied darkness. Sound familiar?"

"Sounds exactly like what the journal described. Of course, without seeing its rune, we can't say for sure."

The boss leaned back and steepled her fingers, looking at him with her glowing eyes through the gaps. "This was a great find."

"I feel like we're missing a lot. What do you want to bet those killers were members of the rebuilt Veiled Cross?"

"You're probably right. It's troubling that followers of the Sword Lord were willing to murder the woman to keep her quiet. It speaks to the seriousness of the danger Umbral Tide represents."

"If the demon's sealed away in their castle, maybe we should just leave things as is. Let them handle protecting it."

The boss sighed. "If only it were so simple. But if there are other elemental orbs out there, the barrier could be breached. And Solomon the Great is far too powerful and skilled to underestimate. He may well find a way to breach the barrier on his own. However good their defenses, they can't compare to our vault."

"Yeah, but how do I get in? A holy barrier will stop Ruq, and if he can't go in, neither can I. Do you want me to use the orb? I can absorb the holy energy then use it to scour the evil out of the castle."

"That's probably our best bet," the boss said. "For now I want you to head out there and take a firsthand look at the barrier. We need a better idea what we're dealing with. I—"

Her phone buzzed midsentence. She glanced at the screen. "Crystal. She found an expert on Crusader weapons. In Cairo."

"Hmm. If he's a member of the new Veiled Cross, this might be a good way to make contact."

"Might be a good way to walk into a trap," the boss said.

"Yeah, but risk is part of the deal. A trap is a good deal less dangerous if you know you're walking into it."

"I'll have Crystal book you an appointment with him."

"Later this afternoon, please. I want to make sure Anatoly is fully with it and have a look around wherever we're meeting."

"Good call. I'll email you the details. Stay safe."

"I'll do my best." Daisuke stood, took a step toward the door, paused, and turned back. "Did you ever meet Branik?"

"No. The archangels can divide their consciousness into thousands of fragments but I never had a chance to speak directly with one of his. In fact, I never spoke with any of the archangels. I was a very low-ranking angel."

"Well, that was his loss. Later, boss." Daisuke headed back to the teleportation chamber. It clearly said something about his mind that the idea of walking into a potential trap with magicproof killers and then visiting a sealed castle with a greater demon inside felt like just another day at the office.

Whether it said something good or bad he had no idea.

CHAPTER TEN

The trip back from Zurich took no longer than the trip there and once again Daisuke found himself in his hotel room, this time a good deal lighter on paperwork. Honestly, if he didn't have to do any reading for the next month, it wouldn't hurt his feelings any.

"If you don't read, how are we going to get our kitchen table cleaned off?" Ruq asked.

"We'll move that junk to the coffee table in the living room if it becomes an issue. Either that or you could read it all."

"Forget I said anything."

Daisuke grinned. Threatening Ruq with work always kept him quiet. And speaking of keeping quiet, he needed to check in with Anatoly. Eighteen hours' sleep should be plenty.

He sent a text and blew out a breath when a reply popped up seconds later. *Awake and ready to go.*

Good. Daisuke crossed the hall and knocked on Anatoly's door. His current partner opened up and waved him in. He moved without any hint of discomfort. Excellent.

"Thanks for warding my door last night," Anatoly said.

"No problem." Daisuke dropped into the room's lone chair. "You didn't look up to company. Especially the dagger-wielding kind. We need to talk. A lot happened while you were out."

Daisuke filled him in on what he found in the papers as well as his meeting this afternoon with the Crusades expert.

When Daisuke finished, Anatoly stared at him, eyes wide. "Wow. Sorry to make you do all the reading by yourself."

Daisuke waved a hand. "Forget about it, I'm used to working alone. I'm supposed to be meeting the expert sometime this afternoon. Are you going to be up to keeping a long-distance eye on things?"

"Yes, I'm fully recovered." Anatoly's brow furrowed. "Perhaps I should go with you. A simple disguise would be enough to let me move around without drawing attention."

"I appreciate the offer, but one person will make him less nervous than two. I just don't want anyone sneaking up on me while we're talking. Or worse, a bunch of cops showing up to arrest the murderer's accomplice."

"Fair enough. I'll follow you the whole way. My spell will also act as a warning. If something disrupts it, you can be sure the killers are nearby."

Daisuke's phone chimed and he glanced at the screen. He had a new email. He tapped the button and sure enough it was from Crystal with details of the meeting.

Anatoly cocked an eyebrow. "News?"

"An update from Crystal. Our expert is a Professor Elias at the University of Cairo. Meeting's at three o'clock, main building, room two." He typed out a quick confirmation and thanks. "That gives me five hours to wander around the campus and see what sort of trouble's waiting."

Daisuke summoned his trunk, pulled out the dagger, and wrapped it in one of his old t-shirts. Next he grabbed his messenger bag and put the dagger into it. Walking around a college campus with a shoulder holster seemed a bit less than subtle, so the pistol went into his bag as well.

Ready as he'd ever be, Daisuke slung the bag over his shoulder. "Wish me luck."

"I don't believe in luck. Be careful."

Daisuke grinned. "Solid plan. Later."

Daisuke slipped out of the room and hurried out of the hotel. Squinting against the glare, he flagged down a battered cab older than he was. He climbed in and pulled the back door shut. "University of Cairo."

With a grunt of confirmation, the cabbie sped away. Daisuke watched the city with no particular interest. He'd visited plenty of places over his years with the Circle and they were all different yet also depressingly familiar. Nice places, bad places, and lots of people just trying to survive while having no idea how close they were to having some supernatural horror devouring them at any given moment. He sometimes envied them their ignorance.

The taxi stopped in front of an open area crisscrossed with sidewalks. Students and faculty bustled between the sand-colored buildings. They wore an odd mixture of modern and old-fashioned clothing. People dressed in everything from sundresses to hijabs to white suits to jeans. It was… something. Unlike a lot of people, Daisuke hadn't loved his school experience, he'd been too bitter about his exile from home.

At least he wasn't a student here, though he could

certainly pass for one, leaving aside the fact that he hadn't seen a single Asian face.

He blew out a breath and focused on the task at hand as he strode down the nearest sidewalk. When he passed each person, invisible tendrils of magic went out. If any of them were magicproof, he'd know at once.

An hour of fruitless wandering later, Daisuke paused in the modest shade of a gnarled olive tree. Sweat trickled down his neck as he surveyed the crowds. He'd found nothing out of the ordinary yet.

A quick check of his phone revealed no messages and that he had three hours to kill before the meeting. Might as well see what he could learn. He spotted a sign with directions to the university museum and headed toward it. If they had some Crusader-era relics or records on display, he might find a clue.

He smiled at the foolish idea. Given how well the order had hidden any information about their true goals, the odds of randomly stumbling on something useful in a museum exhibit hardly bore consideration.

As soon as he stepped inside the museum, Daisuke sighed. Air conditioning at last. The cool, dim interior made a welcome break from the scorching Cairo sun. Daisuke's boots echoed on the polished marble as he strode past glass cases of ancient pottery and stone carvings. His gaze flicked over each museum patron. None of them paid him or his ethereal probes any attention.

Maybe he was overthinking things. This line of work could make you paranoid.

The thought had barely formed when one of his probes fizzled. He traced it to a security guard standing near some pharaoh's golden casket. A second probe met the same fate as the first. It seemed he'd found his first magicproof modern knight. And he was working as a rent-a-cop. Kind of underwhelming.

Daisuke sank onto a bench where he could keep the guard in his peripheral vision and run a few more tests.

You sure that's a good idea? Ruq's telepathic voice appeared in his mind. *He might notice.*

He hasn't yet and even if he does, that will tell us something.

With slow, subtle efforts, he sent probing threads of ether toward the guard to search for the source of his protection. He wore no jewelry, making an artifact unlikely. The barrier or whatever it was emanated evenly from every inch of the man, like his body generated it.

Weird. Donny might understand what it all meant, but Daisuke didn't have a clue. He texted Anatoly and asked if he could see the guard via scrying. A minute later the reply came back negative.

So much for keeping an eye out for the killers that way.

When he'd performed every test he could think of, Daisuke stood and resumed his meander through the exhibition halls. One section had a few fragments of Templar lore and Crusader history, but no earth-shattering revelations, exactly as he expected.

When his meeting time approached, Daisuke left the museum and headed back to the main university building. Before he entered he whispered, "Stay out here and let me know if anyone who looks like a magicproof killer shows up."

"What do they look like?" Ruq asked.

"Soldiers. You shouldn't have any trouble telling them apart from normal students and teachers. If you're not sure, let me know just to be safe."

Ruq launched himself off Daisuke's shoulder to begin patrolling the area. Having his familiar out here made Daisuke feel better given Anatoly's inability to see the killers with his magic.

Precautions taken, Daisuke strode into the lobby where he found a little map of the building. It didn't take long to locate room two. When he arrived, he could just hear a faint voice from inside. Sounded like a class remained in session.

Daisuke slipped through the door and found a seat at the very back. Professor Elias, a slim, middle-aged man with thinning hair and a nice suit, was in the middle of his lecture.

"...and so, in a few short decades, the once-noble Templars degenerated into little more than glorified bankers."

Daisuke raised an eyebrow at the man's disdain. If he was a member of the Veiled Cross, he had little in the way of warm feelings for his ancestors' allies. While the students scribbled notes, Daisuke extended his magical senses over the room. To his relief, neither the pupils nor the professor reacted in any way to his probes.

The professor's droning voice finally fell silent. He ended by saying, "Don't forget to read chapters twelve through fifteen in preparation for Friday's lecture. Class dismissed."

The students gathered their things and filed out of the classroom. Daisuke remained seated, his gaze fixed on the older man. When the final straggler closed the door behind her, Professor Elias focused on Daisuke.

"Mr. Kugo, I presume? You're early."

Daisuke stood and joined him at the front of the class. "What can I say? I couldn't resist the chance to sit in on a lecture. I'm something of a Crusader fan myself. Fascinating time in history."

"Indeed." The professor's eyes narrowed, but his tone remained pleasant. "The young lady I emailed with made mention of a dagger you wanted examined."

Daisuke reached into his bag and pulled out the Veiled Cross dagger, unwrapped it, and held it out hilt first. The professor took it and turned it over in his hands before collecting a magnifying glass from his desk for an even closer look.

After a long moment, he looked up, his expression unreadable. "It's a genuine Veiled Cross dagger. How did you come by this, Mr. Kugo?"

Daisuke shrugged. "An information broker. She's not with us anymore."

The professor's eye twitched so slightly he feared he might've imagined it.

Daisuke had never been great at subtlety. Probably best to come right out and ask. "Are you a member of the new Order of the Veiled Cross, Professor Elias?"

"Did your information broker give you that name as well?"

"I never spoke with her in person. She ran into some thugs in the slum and got her throat cut. Sad to think you can't walk around without fearing for your life."

"She was poking her nose into things best left alone. Warnings were given and ignored."

"And who the fuck are you to give warnings and kill people who ignore them?"

Elias sighed. "I am the current High Warden of the Order of the Veiled Cross. And I'll tell you what I told her. Some things are best left buried. You'll not get a second warning."

"Some things? Like Umbral Tide?"

Elias's face scrunched up. "What?"

Daisuke couldn't contain a laugh, and from his scowl Elias didn't appreciate it. "You don't even know the name of the demon your idiot ancestor Sir Thomas released? Umbral Tide is a greater demon dedicated to Astaroth, Demon Lord of the Undead. I suspect it's now fully free and trapped by the holy barrier the knights created."

"You're better informed than I feared. It seems the time for warnings is past." The professor took the dagger in a fighting grip, the blade laid back against his forearm, and lowered his stance.

Before he could lunge, Daisuke snapped his fingers and bound Elias from head to toe in ethereal chains. "Your pet killers might be a problem for wizards, Professor, but one ordinary old man isn't."

Elias snarled and fought, but he'd have a better chance of breaking chains of steel. When he'd had enough thrashing Elias asked, "Who are you really? One of Ahmed's flunkies?"

"Hardly. Ahmed's dead, I killed him a couple days ago along with about a third of the Spirit Eaters. The Elemental Orb is also locked up for safekeeping. That's what you were really worried about, wasn't it? That orb would've allowed Ahmed to absorb the holy barrier protecting Taba Castle."

"You really are well informed. You're also quite correct. We cared nothing for the woman, but she was determined to help Ahmed and we couldn't allow him to gain access to Taba Castle. When Mustafa acquired the orb we were confident that there was no way for Ahmed to get access. Then Mustafa was killed and the orb stolen despite our security precautions. All our forces rushed to the castle to stop him, but he never showed. Where did you encounter him?"

"Japan. And I'll tell you why. He wanted to gain the power of the elemental shrine there. Likely so he could wipe out your knights or whatever you call them and claim Umbral Tide's power for himself. He seemed like the sort who would be into corrupt power."

"He was, indeed, that sort. So what happens now?"

"I have a lot of questions and I suspect you're just the fellow to answer them."

"I've told you all I care to. If Ahmed is dead, we'll let you go as long as you leave Cairo immediately."

Daisuke shook his head. Talk about arrogant. "You're the one magically bound, not me. Trying to make threats in your current position is kind of pathetic."

"No, killing wizards is what we do. Sir Hugh knew that only a wizard could breach the barrier so he organized the order around that task. My knights will be here soon. Even if you kill me, they'll kill you and my successor will take over the order. There's no way you can win."

Ruq, get down here. Company's on the way.

He sensed Ruq's confirmation and went to the door to let him in. He was three strides away when four men, their faces hidden by cloth masks, burst through the door, daggers leading.

I didn't see them, I swear!

Daisuke ignored Ruq, leapt back, and pulled the pistol out of his bag. Ether flooded his body, enhancing and speeding up his movements. He flicked the safety off, aimed, and shot the nearest killer through the chest.

The man groaned and collapsed.

That shot set the clock running. Someone would be calling the cops any second now.

The three remaining killers charged. With his enhanced senses, Daisuke had no trouble picking off the first two, but the third reached him and slapped the pistol out of his hand.

He drew back for a thrust only to collapse, twitching, when Ruq's stinger slammed into his neck.

"You killed them." Elias's disbelief would've been amusing under different circumstances.

"You don't miss a thing." Daisuke put the pistol away along with the dagger he brought.

His phone chimed with a text from Anatoly. The cops were, indeed, on their way.

"Looks like we're going to have to continue this conversation elsewhere. But first..." Daisuke grabbed one of the new arrival's daggers and stabbed one of the corpses. A thread of ether touched the blood and wavered without breaking. Good.

"You kill them and now you desecrate their bodies? I knew you were evil; the imp just confirms it."

"Hey!" Ruq sounded offended, even though he was, in fact, at least somewhat evil.

Daisuke ignored them both and took a last look around. Satisfied that nothing remained to identify him at the scene, he gestured and Elias floated off the ground. Daisuke pushed him through the nearest shadow onto the shadow paths.

"Branik save me!" Elias said. "Is this Hell?"

Ruq cackled. "Hell? Abaddon's hell is so much worse than this. You humans have no understanding of how nice the mortal realm really is."

"This is the shadow paths," Daisuke said. "Basically a demi-plane connected to every shadow in the world where time largely stops. It's also where I'm going to leave you if you don't start getting more cooperative. Imagine an eternity wandering the endless darkness with no way to escape."

"You're a monster."

"Spare me your self-righteous judgements, you

murdering asshole. The only reason you're still breathing is because I think we both want the same thing, a permanent solution to the situation at Taba Castle. I can help you with that if you'll just let me."

"How can you help?" Elias asked.

Finally, the question Daisuke had been waiting for. "What say we get out of here and discuss it somewhere more pleasant?"

CHAPTER ELEVEN

Daisuke couldn't stop smiling as he remembered the look on Anatoly's face as he thrust Professor Elias at him with a brief introduction before returning to the shadow paths to head for Zurich. Now for the third time this trip he stepped out of the teleportation chamber and walked over to the boss's office. He frowned when he arrived. He couldn't sense her presence. That was rare.

He expanded his awareness and soon found her downstairs. Maybe Crystal needed something. It didn't matter for his purposes. Daisuke headed for the steps and at the bottom found her closing the door to Crystal's computer room.

"I thought I sensed you arrive," the boss said. "Why are you holding a bloody dagger?"

"Professor Elias set me up. Four of the magicproof killers arrived during our chat. Fun fact, he's the current High Warden of the Order of the Veiled Cross and not at all magicproof. Lucky for me, it turns out the killers weren't bulletproof."

"Or poison proof," Ruq added.

"Yeah, Ruq's poison killed one of them no problem. Wouldn't you think imp poison counted as magical?"

"Focus, Daisuke. The dagger?"

"Right. Before I left, I collected a blood sample from one of the dead killers. I figured Donny could use it to try and figure out what makes them magicproof. Assuming I can't convince Elias to tell me." He held the dagger out to her and she took it with a grimace of distaste.

"This is not how blood samples are generally delivered."

"I was in a hurry. After I shot three of the killers, someone called the cops. This seemed like the quickest way to collect the sample."

"Okay, and where is Elias now?" she asked.

"I dumped him off in Anatoly's hotel room. I'm hoping I can convince him that we want the demon sealed away as much as he does. At a minimum he's got to be sick of protecting the castle. It's been nearly a thousand years. I'm surprised the barrier is still holding."

"If they connected it directly to Heaven's power, it'll last until someone destroys it. Do you really think you can bring him around?"

"I don't know, boss. I have options if he's not willing to tell me what I need to know. He's ordered at least one murder and probably more, so I have no qualms about doing whatever I need to in order to extract what he knows. Willing is better, but if I have to crack his skull open to pull the intel out, I won't feel too bad."

The boss scrubbed a hand across her face. "Alright, do what you have to. I'll get this to Donny."

"Thanks, boss. Any word from Helena and Jinx?"

"Their last message said they were heading out to sea to

hunt down the demon. I have no idea how long that might take."

"I'm sure between the two of them they can handle a low tier demon, even if they aren't at full strength. I'd better get back, Anatoly is no doubt anxious for a more in-depth explanation."

"Good luck." She waved him off and Daisuke retreated to the teleportation chamber. He was eager to resume his discussion with Professor Elias. Though whether the professor was equally eager was another matter altogether.

Five minutes after dropping Elias off in Anatoly's room, Daisuke returned. Both men looked up when he appeared out of the shadows. The professor remained wrapped up in Daisuke's binding spell.

"What in the world is going on and why is he here?" Anatoly asked.

Daisuke gave him an update then said, "I have a few more details to work out with the High Warden here."

"You really think he's going to work with us?" Anatoly asked.

"I think that we want the same thing he does, the demon dealt with permanently. If we can all keep that goal in mind —" Daisuke shot Elias a pointed look "—I'm confident we can figure something out. I also wanted to get that blood sample to the boss as quickly as possible so Donny can figure out what makes these guys magicproof. Not that I think it matters all that much for our current mission, but going forward knowing the how and the why would be useful. You should probably call your contact and let them know the dead guys are the ones who killed the information broker."

"That's not technically correct," Elias said. "It was another group who carried out that mission."

Daisuke frowned. "How many teams do you have?"

Elias snorted. "As if I'd tell you that."

Clearly the professor intended to be less helpful than Daisuke had hoped.

"I'll call her and pass along what I can anyway," Anatoly said. "What they choose to do with it is up to them."

While Anatoly got out his phone, Daisuke turned to focus on the professor. "So what do you say to my proposal? We work together to defeat the demon then go our separate ways."

"I'm not sure I trust you not to simply take the demon's power for yourself. You already have a demon familiar. That hardly fills me with confidence about your reliability."

Daisuke rubbed the bridge of his nose. "Ruq's a special case. I've killed more demons than you've seen. And I don't technically even need your help. I'm offering to keep you in the loop as a show of good faith. I could just as easily dump you in Australia and sort things out on my own. But if I do that, I fear I'll end up having to kill a bunch more people who think they're doing the right thing by trying to stop me. I doubt you want that either."

Elias sighed. "I certainly don't. Can you let me out of these chains? I'm clearly no threat to you."

"Sure." Daisuke gestured and the chains vanished. "Better?"

"Yes. I was getting terribly stiff."

Daisuke pointed at the lone chair then sat on the edge of the bed. "Take a load off."

"Thank you." When he'd settled in the professor asked, "Are you truly confident you can destroy the undead as well as the demon?"

"As confident as I can be. I've been at this long enough to know that there're no guarantees. If you're looking for a one hundred percent promise that nothing will go wrong, you're not living in the real world. For all either of us knows, there could be another Elemental Orb out there and whoever has it could show up out of nowhere and release the demon."

"My very fear." Elias's whole face wrinkled as he thought. "So be it. What is it you need from my people?"

"Just for them to stay out of my way. The fewer people I have to worry about, the better."

"I can order the knights on patrol near Taba Castle to pull back to our main base. That will give you clear access."

"Good. Wait, you guys didn't happen to kidnap a pair of archeologists a couple years back, did you?"

"Indeed, those two fools couldn't take a hint either. We have a nonaggression pact with the local freedom fighters. We arranged to trade the scientists for some supplies and weapons while they got the ransom. No one was harmed, but it was made clear that, should they return, things wouldn't end so well for them."

Daisuke was spared having to comment when Anatoly ended his call and said, "The police are working the scene now. Their main concern is Professor Elias's absence. There's a citywide alert out for him."

"If you can return me to the campus, I'll sort things out—tell them I was hiding. Then I'll send orders for a three-day pause in patrols. That should give you plenty of time to do what you have to. Should this work out, your name will go down in our chronicles as the hero who redeemed our ancestors. And if it fails, you'll be remembered as the fool who doomed the world."

Daisuke didn't care what these people thought of him one way or the other, as long as they stayed out of his way. "Let's get you back. The sooner we can deal with Umbral Tide, the better."

Another quick shadow walk returned Elias to the campus.

When Daisuke returned Anatoly asked, "Do you trust him?"

"Not especially, but as long as he gets everyone out of our way, that's good enough for me. If he doesn't, well, we'll deal with that when we have to."

CHAPTER TWELVE

Thirty hours of steady cruising brought the rusted-out trawler within sight of the coordinates Captain Ali had provided. From her spot in the front of the boat, Helena neither saw nor sensed any sign of the demon. The debris floating nearby confirmed that the attack happened, but she found no sign of the creature responsible.

"Do we just cruise around and hope it finds us?" Jinx waved a hand and coughed as the wind shifted, blowing exhaust fumes in their faces.

"That was pretty much always the plan. Only the starting place changed. Though you should change 'cruising around' to 'following a nearby smuggling route.' Captain Demir is supposed to change course to the nearest known route any time now."

Jinx frowned. "Why are there even smuggling routes? We're in the middle of the sea. Ships can go anywhere they want."

"I'm no expert," Helena said. "But it's my understanding

that the big shipping companies use particular routes and those tend to be the areas patrolled by local coast guards and navies. Smuggling routes are just courses of travel which avoid the busy areas."

"Huh. You know, the more time I spend in civilization the stranger some of the details seem."

"I've lived my whole life in civilization and I still find most of it strange. The best advice I can offer is to roll with it. The more you think about the strangeness, the worse your head will hurt." The boat began a slow turn to the right and then they were chugging along again. "Looks like Captain Demir has chosen his new heading."

Jinx wasn't listening to her. Instead she stared into the debris field with a faraway look in her eyes.

"Jinx? Everything okay?"

"Ali was wrong. Most of the people on that ship weren't killed. The psychic residue isn't strong enough. I'd say a dozen people at most died here."

Helena wasn't sensitive enough to psychic auras to confirm Jinx's observation, but she trusted her not to make a random claim. Whether or not it ended up their problem, time would tell. Assuming the demon's master kidnapped them for some reason, they might still be aboard their ship. Freeing them after dealing with the demon shouldn't be too much of a problem.

She directed a humorless smile inwards. Shouldn't be too much of a problem. Talk about famous last words.

The trawler chugged along for a couple more hours, the sea as calm and flat as a sheet of glass. The sun hung high in the sky and hardly a cloud could be seen. Seemed a shame to ruin such a beautiful day with a demon battle, but one was coming. Helena sensed the very faintest hint of corruption headed their way from the northeast.

She squinted against the glare, shading her eyes and scanning the sky. This thing was supposed to be roughly the size of a giant squirrel. Picking it out, even against the blue sky, was no simple feat.

Even though she couldn't see it, the corruption intensified with each passing minute, making her skin crawl.

"It's coming," Helena said.

"I feel it too." Jinx pointed at an empty section of sky about half a mile to their left. "It's right there. Probably invisible."

Helena narrowed her eyes, focusing on the patch of sky Jinx indicated. She activated a detect invisibility spell and sure enough a shimmering distortion indicated the demon's location. It circled overhead as if not certain what to do about them.

"What's it waiting for?" Jinx asked.

"Orders from its master would be my guess. The damn thing's too high for my magic to reach and I can't fly. Do you have anything that might work?"

Jinx shook her head. "My shadows can't fly. Could we do something to lure it into attacking?"

"Anything we try is liable to alert the master that there are wizards aboard this ship, which might be enough to convince him to recall the demon and hightail it out of the area. Much as I hate it, I think we'll need to be patient."

Helena gritted her teeth, frustration mounting as the minutes ticked by and the demon continued to circle them. It took all her self-control not to try something, anything, to bring the creature down. But she knew they couldn't risk spooking it, not when they were so close.

An hour of cruising later, Captain Demir stuck his head out of the wheelhouse. "I'm picking up another boat on radar. She's running without a transponder, same as us."

Maybe this was what the demon had been waiting for. "Where is it?" Helena asked.

Demir pointed almost dead ahead. "She ain't moving. It's like they want us to approach. Might be someone in trouble. What do you want to do?"

"Keep going. Slow and steady." Helena shaded her eyes and thought she could see a dark spot in the distance. "Maybe they've seen something useful."

Or maybe they're setting an ambush. She didn't add that last bit, just as she hadn't informed the crew that the demon was circling them. The men couldn't do anything about it and their panic wouldn't be helpful.

The captain nodded and closed the wheelhouse window.

"Get ready," Helena said. "If the master is aboard that ship, this'll be the perfect time for the demon to attack."

Jinx clenched her fist. "Let's get this over with. The waiting is killing me."

Helena knew just how she felt. Daisuke always liked to joke before a fight—it kept him loose—but Helena didn't have that in her.

Ten minutes more brought the unmoving ship into view.

It bobbed listlessly on the waves, its deck empty, with no sign of the crew. But they were there; Helena sensed their life forces.

What were they playing at?

Her answer came a moment later when the demon suddenly dove, its invisibility melting away to reveal a monstrous form that did, indeed, look like a black-furred giant flying squirrel with a skull head and long, razor-sharp claws.

It flew past the ship and spat a line of hellfire in front of them before soaring back out of range.

Helena cursed. She'd expected it to fly right at them and had raised an invisible barrier to stop its attack. Jinx hadn't done any better, not managing to get off a single spell.

"It's fast," Jinx said.

That was the understatement of the year. Not that they had time to dwell on it. On the other ship, half a dozen men armed with machine guns had boiled up on deck. In the middle of the group stood a single, unarmed man dressed all in black and wearing a ring that pulsed with corruption. He had to be the demon's master.

"Surrender," the master said. "Or my pet will roast the lot of you alive."

He said that as if the alternative was apt to be better. The wheelhouse window slammed open. "What do we do?" Demir asked.

"Put the boat in neutral and get below deck," Helena said. "We'll handle this and tell you when it's safe."

Thankfully, Demir didn't argue, and soon his head vanished into the galley.

"You take the master and his thugs, I'll block the demon and stray bullets," Helena said.

"I said surrender!" the master shouted. "Come out on deck this instant, unarmed, or burn!"

Helena led the way around to the opposite side of the boat so they were visible. As soon as the master saw them his eyes went wide.

"Now!" Helena said.

Jinx pointed and clawed, shadowy arms emerged from

the enemy soldiers' shadows, wrapping them up as they fired uselessly into the air.

"Kill them!" the master shouted a moment before a hand appeared from his shadow and ripped his throat out.

The demon went berserk.

It dove, spewing hellfire that splashed against Helena's golden shield. Before it could climb back into the sky, Jinx sent a stream of shadowy flames roaring out, hammering it dead center and driving it into the side of the enemy ship.

Helena added a golden lance of her own and between them the death glider soon melted into a puddle of black goo that slid into the sea.

"We did it!" Jinx said.

"We sure did. That thing was much weaker than the claw demon we fought in Odessa."

"Yeah, the hardest part was getting close enough to hit it." Jinx nodded toward the shadow bound thugs. "I left them alive in case you wanted to ask about the coast guard sailors."

"Good. I was hoping you would." Helena concentrated and a hand made of golden energy reached across the gap separating the two ships. Her magical construct dragged one of the thugs over to her. He landed with a thud on deck. "I have some questions."

"Fuck you, bitch!"

Helena winced and shook her head. That was about as good a start as she'd expected.

"Want me to encourage him?" Jinx asked.

"I was hoping to avoid that, but I suppose you'd better."

Jinx made a fist and the shadows tightened until Helena could hear the prisoner's bones creaking. It wouldn't take much more for them to start breaking.

"Okay, that's enough for now," Helena said. The shadows

relaxed and the man let out a loud sigh of relief. "Shall we try this again? Please understand that I won't stop her next time until your ribs shatter."

The prisoner blanched and she felt confident he better understood his position.

"Now, where are the coast guard sailors you kidnapped?"

"We sold them in the Kostova slave market. It was easy money. Once the demon finished with them they didn't have any fight left."

"Hey!" Helena turned to see Demir emerge from the wheelhouse. "I thought you said you'd let us know when it was safe?"

"I intended to. I just wanted to finish questioning this prisoner first. Can you contact Captain Ali? I've got some news that will please him."

"Why don't we just go back and you can talk to him face to face? The demon's dead, right? We're finished here."

Helena stared him down. "Humor me. A few more minutes isn't going to make any difference."

Demir threw up his hands. "Fine. I don't know why I try to talk sensibly to you. Even wizard women are still women. Come up to the wheelhouse and we'll try the satellite phone."

Helena and Jinx shared a smile and followed him up to the wheelhouse. Once he realized he couldn't intimidate them into bed, Demir had mellowed into an exasperated annoyance which she considered a vast improvement.

Helena and Jinx squeezed into the cramped wheelhouse and watched as Demir fiddled with a yellow brick of a satellite phone, cursing under his breath as he attempted to get a signal. After several long moments he dialed a number.

"Captain Ali? This is Demir. Your wizards wish to speak with you."

Demir held out the phone and Helena took it. "Ali, it's Helena. The demon is dead and we've captured several members of the smuggler crew. All your sailors weren't killed in the attack. Turns out they were sold in the Kostova slave market. I don't know much about criminal networks in this part of the world, but it's a place for you to start."

"I am sadly all too familiar with it. Your news is both welcome and troublesome. Kostova is across the border and I have no jurisdiction there. And to say that the Bulgarian government, such as it is, will be of no help would be to vastly understate their disdain."

"That's most unfortunate, Captain. What would you like us to do with the prisoners?"

"Bring them back. They'll be interrogated before trial and execution."

"Understood. We'll see you in a day or so." Helena hung up. She wished she could do something for the kidnapped men, but it was a matter for the proper authorities. There wasn't even any magic involved, at least not as far as she was aware.

"A quick question if you don't mind," Demir said.

"Go ahead," Helena said.

"Would it be okay if we searched the other ship for salvage? It would be a shame to leave anything valuable behind."

"Be my guest," Helena said. "But I thought you were in a hurry to get out of here?"

"I was. But as you were talking with the good Captain Ali I had time to think. Though we will receive our pardons, we'll be starting over with nothing. Even a few thousand Euros' worth of salvage would help us make a new beginning."

"I can't fault your logic. If your men drag the other prisoners over here and put them somewhere, we'll call it even."

"We have no brig," Demir said.

"Don't worry," Jinx said. "Once you get them where they're going, I'll bind them with shadow webs. They won't be going anywhere until I allow it."

Demir offered a little bobbing bow, the grimace of distaste kind of ruining the effect. "As you say. We'll get started."

Helena and Jinx left the men to their work. Though they'd finished the job, Helena couldn't help feeling they'd only half done it. Rescuing those kidnapped sailors fell to the Turkish government, but she resolved to ask the boss about it when she reported in.

CHAPTER THIRTEEN

The ancient pickup groaned as it bounced across another ridge of sunbaked rock. Daisuke gripped the handle above the passenger side window, his scarred right arm aching from the constant vibration. Sand and grit had worked its way into every crevice of the truck's cab despite the windows being rolled up. His work for the Circle had taken him to some miserable places, but this bleak landscape easily competed for the least hospitable.

An endless expanse of sand and rock stretched to the horizon in every direction, broken only by the occasional scraggly bush or twisted piece of metal, remnants of old wars scattered across the peninsula. He couldn't begin to imagine how anyone lived out here.

"I fear the truck might overheat," Anatoly said from his position behind the wheel.

"I'm more worried about us overheating. We've got to be getting close." He checked the GPS app on his phone. Assuming it was working right, they had about ten miles to go before they reached the coordinates Crystal provided.

"Humans are such weaklings," Ruq said. "This wouldn't even count as a warm day in Abaddon's hell."

The truck lurched and the suspension creaked in protest as Anatoly steered them around a jutting boulder. Ahead of them the sun beat down mercilessly, sending heat shimmering into the air and creating mirages as they pressed deeper into the wasteland. Even with the air conditioning running full blast, sweat trickled down Daisuke's back.

He checked the GPS again. "Stop here. We're getting close and I want to make sure we don't drive into an ambush."

Anatoly pulled the truck to a halt in the lee of a wind-carved rock formation. Little separated this section of nothing from all the other nothing they'd been driving through.

"Want me to fly around and take a look?" Ruq asked.

"No, I don't want you getting too close to the barrier. That holy magic will be as hard on you as it is on Umbral Tide." Daisuke got his phone out. "We'll have Crystal check it out with the satellite."

Daisuke dialed Crystal's extension and after two rings she said, "Daisuke? What's up?"

Her voice came through clearly despite their remote location. He found that almost as unbelievable as an invisible castle. "We're two miles out, approaching from the west. I wanted to confirm that we were in the clear."

"One sec." The faint tapping of computer keys came from the speaker. "I see you guys. There's nothing moving within twenty miles of the target. You're good to approach."

"Great, what about a fallback position where we can make camp?"

"There's an oasis about three miles north of the target. I

don't know how good the water source is, but it's unoccupied."

"Perfect, thanks." Daisuke ended the call and nodded to Anatoly. "We're clear."

Anatoly shifted the truck into gear and they continued their slow progress through the wasteland. Daisuke closed his eyes, letting his magical senses extend outward. The barrier's presence grew stronger with each passing yard.

A few minutes later, Anatoly brought them to a stop. "That's two miles. We must be close. The holy magic is like a flare in my magical senses."

"Mine too." Daisuke opened his eyes. To his normal vision, nothing but sand and rock stretched before them. But his magical sight revealed a dome of white light anchored to the earth in five places. That matched the description he'd read in Sir Hugh's journal.

"Should we get out for a closer look?" Anatoly asked.

"To hell with that. I can look just fine from the cab. Drive slowly around the perimeter and stop when I say."

Anatoly eased the truck forward, keeping a steady distance from the barrier's edge. Through his magical sight, Daisuke studied the dome's structure. The holy magic pulsed with a steady rhythm, like a heartbeat. Five anchor points held it in place, each one marked by an especially dense collection of divine energy. He found it remarkable that men were willing to give their lives so easily. Faith was a terrifying thing.

"Wait," Daisuke said. "Something's wrong. Stop here."

The truck stopped a few feet from the third anchor. Faint black lines were running through it. Everything still looked strong, but eventually those flaws would cause the barrier to shatter. And when it did, Umbral

Tide would be free. Not a prospect anyone living would relish.

They continued their survey and found minor damage at one other anchor. Daisuke had seen enough. "Let's head for the oasis Crystal mentioned. Then I need to return to base to talk to the boss."

Anatoly guided them away from the barrier. A five-minute drive brought them to an oasis which proved to be little more than a depression in the ground with a few struggling date palms clustered around a brackish pool. Still, it beat camping in the open desert. Daisuke helped Anatoly set up a simple two-man tent while Ruq lounged in the sun, lying on his back in rat form like a cat on a windowsill.

Daisuke finished securing the last tent stake. "I have to head for home. Will you be okay here?"

Anatoly nodded. "No problem. Despite the heat it is very peaceful."

"Yeah, all the terrorists must be on vacation. I shouldn't be long. Come on, Ruq, time to go."

The imp transformed from rat form into a bat-winged humanoid and flew to Daisuke's shoulder. "Finally. Will we have time to get cookies?"

"No, strictly business this visit."

"Come on. That barrier isn't going to break right away. We can spare an hour."

"No snacks this trip. When Umbral Tide is dealt with we can get ice cream."

"Deal," Ruq said.

There weren't a ton of shadows to choose from so Daisuke ended up sinking into the one cast by their truck. A quick walk down the shadow paths brought him to the Circle's teleportation chamber.

He went to the boss's office and knocked.

"Come in, Daisuke." He entered to find her desk covered with papers, the very same ones he'd deposited there on his last visit if he wasn't mistaken. "This is some interesting reading. What did you think of the barrier?"

"It's failing," he said. "Not quickly, but two of the anchor points already show signs of degradation. I suspect in a century or so it'll collapse completely."

"So it's a problem, but not an imminent one."

"Exactly. The only question left is, do you want me to deal with it now or do we leave it for some future Circle member?"

Angelique leaned back in her chair, steepling her fingers as she considered Daisuke's question. Her golden eyes narrowed. "If we leave it, there's always the risk that someone else will break the barrier before then to claim Umbral Tide's power for themselves."

Daisuke nodded. "Solomon the Great comes to mind. Plus whatever other evil assholes might be lurking about. Better to deal with this now."

"Agreed. Get the Elemental Orb out of the vault and do what you have to."

"Okay, boss. Fingers crossed this goes the way we're hoping."

"I second that. Best of luck."

CHAPTER FOURTEEN

Daisuke emerged from the shadow of the rented truck, the desert sun nearly blinding him after the dimness of the shadow paths. He blinked, waiting for his eyes to adjust. When his vision cleared, he saw Anatoly resting in the shade of the oasis palms, a wet towel over his head.

As Daisuke approached, the Russian sat up and tossed the towel aside. "That was fast. I take it the boss wants this handled now?"

"Yup." Daisuke held up the Elemental Orb. "She wants us to go in and deal with Umbral Tide before someone with bad intentions shows up."

Anatoly stood and brushed the sand from his clothes. "I suppose there's no point in putting it off. Did she give you any special instructions?"

"Just to do what we have to do." Daisuke shrugged. "I figure we'll use the orb to absorb the barrier and then we'll go inside and scope out the situation."

"You want me to come with you?"

Daisuke nodded. “Without the barrier, who knows what might come out of there. I’ll have Ruq keep an eye on things from on high. I don’t want him too close when I’m throwing holy energy around. You okay with that?”

“Sure, no problem,” Anatoly said. “I’m not certain how much I can add in a fight, but I’m willing to give it my best shot.”

“Perfect. Let’s go.” Daisuke climbed into the truck and Anatoly slid behind the wheel.

As the truck bounced over the rough terrain, Daisuke considered the task ahead. He had no way of making a proper plan without knowing exactly what they might find inside. A really strong demon and some undead knights seemed like the minimum, but given what he knew about the knights’ collection of corrupt artifacts, assuming they wouldn’t find any other nasty surprises seemed optimistic.

Anatoly pulled the truck to a stop a hundred yards from the barrier and killed the engine. Daisuke climbed out and Ruq immediately flew as high as his link to Daisuke would allow. Normally he liked having his familiar close by to watch his back, but not this time.

Daisuke approached the barrier, holding the orb in front of him. Five feet away, a white glow appeared as it gradually shimmered into view. Daisuke took a deep breath and pressed the orb against the barrier.

Immediately the holy energy flowed into it. The process took about thirty seconds, then the castle stood revealed, ancient stone walls rising to meet the cloudless sky. The lowered portcullis appeared as pristine as the day the smith forged it. In fact the whole castle looked like it had been built last week rather than last millennium.

Any second he expected a wave of darkness to come

rushing out to consume them, but Umbral Tide seemed disinclined to make an appearance.

"Can you raise the portcullis?" Daisuke asked. "I need to get the staff."

While Anatoly raised his hand and wrestled the heavy iron portcullis up out of sight, Daisuke summoned his trunk and pulled the Staff of Law out. The two men hurried through the opening before the portcullis crashed back to earth. No quick getaway today.

A wide dirt courtyard greeted them, its sole occupants a trio of corpses dressed in Crusader armor. Across the killing field the keep proper waited. No doubt the demon and its minions lurked inside.

"Daisuke." Anatoly pointed at the bodies.

They twitched like someone was running an electrical current through them. One by one they rose to their feet, eye sockets glowing with unholy red light. They made perfect targets to test the orb.

Daisuke held it up and focused his will. A beam of white light shot out, engulfing the nearest corpse. An instant later it crumbled to dust. Two more precise blasts dealt with the others the same way. That hadn't used enough of the stored energy to say so.

"I expected them to be tougher," Anatoly said.

"Don't complain, fate might take it personally. Let's check the keep. Stay close. If I have to create a shield, smaller is better."

They crossed the courtyard, Anatoly a step behind Daisuke. Up close, the keep looked just as pristine as the outer walls. The heavy wooden door swung open at Daisuke's touch, revealing a dimly lit interior. He conjured a ball of holy light and sent it floating ahead of them.

The entrance led to a great hall, its floor covered in a thick layer of dust. High-backed wooden chairs lined the long trestle tables on either side of the room. At the far end, a dais supported a throne-like chair. That seemed a bit extravagant for an order of holy knights.

"Can you get any sense of where it's hiding?" Daisuke asked. "Between the background corruption and the orb's power, I can't sense anything more than three feet from me."

Anatoly closed his eyes, but after a few moments he shook his head. "Sorry, I'm not sensing anything specific and I don't dare lose my focus enough to try scrying."

"Good call. I guess we do this the hard way."

Two doors led out of the great hall and Daisuke went right. A long passage ran for as far as he could see. A couple of doors broke up the monotony of dark stone. Daisuke tensed as Anatoly prepared to grab the handle of the nearest.

The door slammed open, revealing what was likely an office of some sort back in the day. Happily no undead called the room home. The second door hid an equally uninteresting storage area.

Daisuke wasn't sure how long they spent searching the first floor, but by the time they finished and found the steps to the dungeon, he wanted the demon to show up just to break the monotony.

"I assumed we'd be fighting more," Anatoly said.

"I imagine we will be once we get downstairs. Evil things, at least in my experience, seem to like living underground. I'm not sure why that should be, but it is."

Daisuke led the way down the narrow stone steps, the orb's glow lighting the way. The air grew colder and damper and the aura of corruption thicker the farther they descended. By the time they reached the bottom, Daisuke's breath puffed out in little clouds. The chill felt almost shocking after the desert heat.

The dungeon consisted of a single long corridor lined with cells on either side. Most of the doors hung open, revealing nothing but dust and the occasional rat skeleton inside. At the far end waited a set of double doors stained nearly black by corruption.

"That has to be it," Daisuke said. "Be ready for anything."

Anatoly nodded and they approached the doors together. Dozens of carved holy symbols decorated the doors. Or they used to. Someone had defaced each of them with deep gouges.

Daisuke reached for the handle, but before he could touch it, the doors swung open on their own. Beyond them lay a large circular chamber, its walls lined with alcoves. In the center of the room stood a knight clad in black armor, a sword strapped to his waist and a grinning skull in place of his face.

Pure darkness surrounded the knight. Though he couldn't separate the demon from the background darkness, he assumed it had to be Umbral Tide.

"Welcome, intruders," the undead knight said. "I am the High Warden of the Order of the Veiled Cross. I don't know how you brought down the cursed barrier, but I thank you. In gratitude, I offer one chance to join us and serve Astaroth."

"I'm going to have to pass on that," Daisuke said. "You're a traitor to the human race and your fellow knights, Sir Thomas. Your place in Astaroth's hell is well earned."

The undead knight's jaw worked silently for a moment. "Why can't any of you understand? The order was wrong, all the orders were wrong. All those years we wasted fighting demons when we could've been working with them. Growing stronger."

He clenched his skeletal hands into fists moments before his body began shuddering. The armor rattled, black smoke pouring from the joints. It looked like Umbral Tide had heard enough of its puppet ranting. For once Daisuke agreed with a demon.

Daisuke conjured a barrier around the room to keep the demon from escaping.

A stream of dark flames erupted from Sir Thomas's outstretched hands.

Daisuke thrust the orb forward. White light blazed forth, forming a wall of holy energy in front of him and Anatoly. The dark flames splashed against the barrier, dissipating into harmless smoke.

Sir Thomas drew his sword, the blade wreathed in unholy flames. He charged, bringing the weapon down in an overhead strike that made Daisuke's wall ring like a bell.

"Do you see the prison?" Daisuke asked.

"No. It could be in any of those niches, but the darkness is blocking them. Why isn't the demon attacking us directly?"

"Don't give it any ideas." The sword crashed down again. The noise was giving Daisuke a headache.

When the blade went up again, Daisuke lashed out with a blast of holy energy that reduced Sir Thomas's head to dust. His body kept hacking away like nothing happened.

Snarling his annoyance, Daisuke blasted twice more until nothing remained of the body. Darkness closed in around them. He transformed the wall into a bubble and not a moment too soon. Umbral Tide began pounding on the shield from all sides.

"This isn't going very well," Anatoly said.

"No kidding. At this rate it's going to smash through my bubble in minutes. I need to go on offense. Can you block any tendrils that get through?"

"I can try. I've never fought a demon this powerful before."

"Try hard."

Daisuke took a deep breath and focused his will through the orb. Holy energy radiated outward in waves of pure white light. Where it struck the darkness, Umbral Tide's essence burned away. The demon pulled back from the holy power's searing touch.

A small tendril of darkness tried to sneak past, but Anatoly blasted it to motes with a lightning bolt.

The orb grew warm as Daisuke poured more power into his attack. Inch by inch the darkness retreated, revealing more of the chamber. Several of the alcoves came into view, but none held the bronze prison.

Sweat rolled down Daisuke's face as he maintained the pressure. The orb's glow dimmed as the stored energy drained away far too quickly for Daisuke's comfort.

Umbral Tide fought back, sending tendrils of darkness stabbing through gaps in Daisuke's expanding sphere of light. Anatoly blasted or deflected them before they could strike home.

"I can't keep this up much longer," Anatoly said.

Daisuke knew how he felt. The orb's power continued to fade. More of the chamber came into view, but still no sign of the prison. His arms trembling with the effort, Daisuke shifted the holy energy from powering the barrier which sealed the dungeon to attack.

Even with that, he didn't have enough energy to finish the job.

Lucky for them Umbral Tide didn't appreciate the precariousness of their position. The remaining darkness exploded upwards, tearing through the ceiling and eventually blowing out through the keep as it fled.

Daisuke hit his knees and checked the orb. Every drop of holy energy had been drained. If the demon had stuck around for even five more seconds they would've had it. On the plus side, he'd burned away over half of its demonic essence.

The first battle ended a draw. Not the result he'd hoped for, but far better than a loss. Anatoly walked over to one of the niches nearest the back wall and returned holding the prison and seal.

"What now?" Anatoly asked.

"Now we finish the job. That battle badly weakened Umbral Tide. I can use the seal to track it down wherever it's gone. Sealing it back inside its prison should be easier given how much damage it took. Right now I need to rest. Can you gather up the artifacts and load them into my trunk?"

"Not a problem."

Anatoly got to work while Daisuke leaned against the wall and collected himself. Eight courses of dessert and twelve hours' sleep would be welcome, but he didn't dare take that much time. He'd settle for an MRE and four hours. Then they'd have to get busy hunting down the demon.

Master, you're about to have company.

Daisuke grimaced. *What sort of company?*

He concentrated and merged his sight with Ruq's. A mix of trucks and other vehicles, some of them with heavy machine guns mounted on the back, were pulling up to the castle's outer wall. The lead truck stopped and a figure in dark robes, his face covered with a head wrap, stepped out and looked the castle over.

A moment later he pulled the wrap down, revealing Elias's face. What the hell was the professor doing here? And what happened to keeping his people away for another couple days? Daisuke didn't have time to explain things right now. He also didn't have the energy to move.

If Elias was in a hurry, he could come down here.

What do you want me to do?

Just watch them for now. If they approach the keep let me know.

"Ruq says Elias and his merry band of killers just rolled up."

Anatoly dropped a Kris-bladed dagger into the trunk. "That wasn't the plan."

"It certainly wasn't. Once I'm recovered we'll see what he wants."

Anatoly grunted and got back to work. Daisuke rubbed his eyes and sighed. Elias was a problem he didn't need right now. Whatever the professor wanted had best be important.

CHAPTER FIFTEEN

Angelique shuffled through the stack of papers on her desk, quickly scanning each document Daisuke had taken from the information broker. She'd read them once already but wanted to go over them again to make sure she hadn't missed anything important. So far she felt confident she hadn't. Pity the woman had gotten herself killed. She might've made a good Circle agent.

Angelique was about to open the journal when her phone rang. Helena—hopefully she had good news. "Go ahead."

"Boss, we just got back to port. The death glider's dead."

"Your tone implies there's bad news."

"Unfortunately some members of the Turkish coast guard ended up captured and sold to a slave market in Kostova. Captain Ali requested our help in recovering them due to cross-border issues. I promised to ask but told him not to get his hopes up."

Angelique leaned back in her chair. "You both did well, but rescuing those sailors, nice as it would be, isn't our concern. Turkish special forces are quite talented. If they want their people back, I'm confident they'll have no trouble extracting them."

"I figured you'd say that. Ali is quite pleased we dealt with the demon, so I doubt he'll give us any trouble. Do you want us to come straight back to Zurich?"

"Yes. Daisuke and Anatoly have things under control in Egypt, for the moment at least, but I want you both rested and ready to provide backup should that become necessary."

"Understood, boss. We should be in tonight. See you then."

"You can go straight home," Angelique said. "Tomorrow morning is soon enough to make your full report. You've certainly earned the rest."

"I won't complain. See you tomorrow." Helena disconnected and Angelique set her phone back on her desk.

That checked one problem off her list. It came as a considerable relief to not have to worry about any more bound demons. Hopefully none of the other demon cults got the bright idea to copy the Devil Man. Not that it could be easily done without Remi's expertise.

She reached for the journal for a second time when her computer chimed. She muttered unkind things and debated ignoring the email before sighing and wiggling her mouse. When the screensaver vanished she found Donny's preliminary analysis of the dead killer's blood. She clicked print.

Once the papers emerged, she grabbed them and started reading. She didn't fully understand all the technical details, but after three years she'd finally gotten him trained to include an executive summary. She skipped to that.

The subjects weren't actually magicproof.

Well that was a hell of a first sentence given that it contradicted everything she'd heard so far. Not that

Angelique would question Donny's analysis. Despite his quirks, he knew his business better than anyone she'd ever met.

The reality is that they're so filled with corruption, it acts like a demonic aura, turning aside weak spells. The blood sample contained traces of powdered Hell-forged black iron. This likely explains how nonwizards could generate such a powerful aura. On the positive side, that much black iron in their blood will prove fatal to an ordinary human in six months to a year.

Angelique frowned at the paper. No way did Anatoly or Daisuke fail to notice a corrupt aura strong enough to repel basic spells. That meant some sort of masking magic, or more likely an item hid it.

More importantly, why did supposedly holy knights inject themselves with powdered black iron? You could only get the stuff from one of the nine hells. Assuming they didn't find a source already on Earth, that meant the people Daisuke made a deal with were, in reality, most likely demon worshippers of some sort.

She had to warn him.

Angelique grabbed her phone and hit his contact number. No signal. An attempted text suffered a similar fate.

She cursed in a very unangelic way. Daisuke and Anatoly were likely walking straight into a trap and she had no way to reach them.

Jinx stared out the side window of Ali's car as they drove through Istanbul on their way to the airport. She could've carried Helena through the shadow paths, but her partner didn't like being carried and the jet had to fly back to Zurich anyway. Jinx quite liked flying, so she had no intention of complaining.

It would be good to get home, though knowing Daisuke was away made her return much less exciting than it would've been. She missed spending time with him and hoped they'd get to partner up again once he completed his current mission.

Istanbul, on the other hand, she would happily leave behind. Something in the air here made her nose tickle and she always felt on the verge of a sneeze. A half-demon with allergies struck her as too ludicrous.

"Hey," Helena said. "Penny for your thoughts."

"Just thinking how nice it'll be to get home."

"You said it. I need a bubble bath in the worst way. Nothing else seems to get the demon stink out."

"I don't think you smell like demons." Jinx turned her head a fraction and sniffed her shoulder. Did she smell like demons?

Helena laughed. "It's the memory of the smell I'm trying to get out of my head. An hour soaking in the tub with a good novel always does the trick after a long mission. And man has this been a long one. I can't remember the last time I had back-to-back jobs. I don't know how Daisuke keeps going the way he does."

"I think he's built differently than the average human." When she realized how that might be interpreted Jinx hastened to add, "Psychologically, I mean."

"I know what you meant." Helena's tone held a hint of amusement. It was nice that they could talk like this. Jinx had been afraid that, since they both liked Daisuke, they wouldn't be able to be friends as well. "He's—"

Jinx's phone rang, interrupting their conversation. Only

four people had her number and one of them was sitting beside her. That meant it had to be Daisuke, Vixen, or the boss.

She hit connect and said, "Hello, boss."

"Jinx, can you find Daisuke when you're on the shadow paths? It's urgent I get a message to him and his phone has no signal."

"Sure, I can find him. I've gotten very familiar with his magical signature."

"Great. Find him and tell him the Order of the Veiled Cross is not to be trusted. They're using Hell-forged black iron to make themselves magic resistant. Tell him to contact me as soon as he has a signal so I can give him a full briefing. Hurry, Jinx."

"Yes, ma'am."

"What's going on?" Helena asked.

Jinx ignored her for the moment and turned to Ali. "Pull over, please. Near a shadow if possible."

"Jinx?" Helena asked.

"The boss asked me to take a message to Daisuke. I don't really understand what it means, but I think he's in trouble."

"Take me with you."

"I can't. I don't have enough power to maintain both of us on the paths and search for Daisuke."

Helena looked like she wanted to argue. Jinx understood how she felt. Had their positions been reversed, she would've wanted to come as well, but as much as Jinx would've liked to bring her along, it really was impossible.

Ali finally found a place to park and Jinx hopped out. A building not that far away cast a perfect shadow.

"Good luck!" Helena shouted after her.

Jinx waved and vanished onto the paths. Now for the

tricky bit. Unlike a human, Jinx's demon blood allowed her to do things here a regular wizard would find impossible. Specifically, she could visit places she'd never been before as long as she knew how to get there, as well as locate someone familiar to her.

Jinx turned south and moved along as quickly as she could while searching. She extended her magical senses, searching for Daisuke's unique magical signature, a mix of dark magic and very human warmth. The paths twisted around her as she moved, responding to her will and desire to find him.

What seemed like minutes here equaled only moments in the real world. Even so she felt the passage of time keenly as she hurried through the darkness.

There! A flicker of familiar energy caught her attention. She homed in on it. Daisuke's presence burned like a dark flame. She was close.

Jinx picked up speed, practically flying now as she raced toward him. The closer she got, the stronger his signature became, pulling her forward like a beacon.

She peeked out of the nearest shadow and watched him and another man she'd never met cross an open stretch of dirt toward a collection of heavily armed soldiers. When she tried to touch them with her magic, it slipped off. These had to be the people she was supposed to warn him about.

Jinx cursed her slowness. If she'd been even a minute quicker she could've arrived before it was too late. Now she'd have to bide her time and be ready to help should the worst happen.

CHAPTER SIXTEEN

Daisuke blew out a long breath and pushed away from the wall. A corruption-soaked dungeon didn't make for the nicest napping place, but at least he no longer felt on the verge of fainting. Elias had made no move to approach the keep, though he and his men had moved into the courtyard and set up three heavy-duty machine guns, which they pointed at the entrance. While Daisuke still had no idea what the man had in mind, it seemed safe to assume his intentions were ill.

He glanced at Anatoly, who sat on Daisuke's trunk, eyes closed and dozing. The Russian looked a bit pale but otherwise recovered. Time to see what their supposed temporary ally wanted.

Daisuke crossed the room and shook Anatoly's shoulder. "Hey. Time to go have a chat with our friend upstairs."

Anatoly cracked one eye open. His pale face had the pinched look of someone fighting off a headache. "Must we? Perhaps Umbral Tide will return and wipe them out."

"Doubtful. It's been four hours and Ruq has seen no sign

of the demon, luckily for us. What he has seen is Elias and his soldiers setting up defensive positions with heavy machine guns targeting the keep door. Not exactly what I'd expect from an ally, even a temporary one."

Anatoly heaved himself up. His legs wobbled for a moment before steadying. "I always thought they were too quick to kill for holy men."

Daisuke laughed. "Have you not read the history of the Crusades? Holy knights had many faults, but a hesitation to kill was never one of them. These clowns look like they're following in the footsteps of their ancestors. So are you good?"

"As good as I'm going to be absent a week of recovery. Want me to handle defense and you can attack?"

"I'm hoping it won't come to that, but if it does, a double-layered barrier would probably be best. You handle outer and I'll take inner. Once they're out of bullets we can decide our next move."

Daisuke shrank the trunk back to card form and tucked it away in his wallet. He kept the Staff of Law in hand. If it came to a fight, the small power boost it offered would be welcome.

Daisuke led the way up the stairs with Anatoly close behind. The keep's interior remained dim despite the afternoon sun, with only thin shafts of light penetrating through arrow slits carved into the thick stone walls.

The entrance hall stretched before them, dust motes dancing in the air. The keep had lost much of its creepy feeling now that Daisuke had destroyed or driven away the demon and undead. No doubt it would never be a comfortable place for humans, but at least it didn't turn his stomach anymore.

Daisuke paused for a moment at the heavy door. An effort of will conjured a wall in front of them. A moment later Anatoly's wall appeared in front of his. The double barrier would turn aside an RPG blast, much less small-arms fire.

With their defenses in place, they stepped out into the sunlight. The glare forced Daisuke to blink a few times. When his eyes had adjusted to the harsh desert glare he looked around the courtyard. Everything looked the same as the last time he checked through Ruq's eyes. Three machine gun nests faced the keep's entrance, manned by soldiers in dark clothing, their faces covered by black cloths. Elias stood behind the center position. He'd swapped his tailored suit for a flowing black robe. Not at all the sort of thing you'd expect the leader of a knightly order to wear.

At least no one opened fire. Daisuke had feared a more aggressive welcome.

"Let's meet them partway," Daisuke said. "Don't lower the barrier."

"I had no intention of doing so."

They strode to the middle of the yard, halfway between the wall and the keep. When they were in place Daisuke shouted, "Come join us, Elias. Just you."

Elias strode forward without a trace of fear or hesitation, his black robes billowing in the desert wind. Daisuke's grip tightened on his staff. Something felt wrong. Why go to all this trouble only to step away from your secure position?

The professor stopped a few feet away and crossed his arms. "Did you defeat the demon?"

"No, but we drove it off and destroyed its undead creations." Daisuke kept his voice neutral. "My next move is to track it down and return it to its prison before it recovers."

Elias shook his head, a cold smile playing across his lips. "No. What you're going to do is hand over the seal and prison."

Daisuke cocked his head. "And why would I do that?"

Elias indicated the many armed men behind him. "I have you a bit outnumbered and all of them are untouchable by magic. There is a limit to how long even wizards can last under a hail of gunfire, and we brought many bullets with us."

"You're not magicproof," Daisuke said. "And as soon as the first bullet flies, I'm killing you. Anyway, none of this is necessary. Umbral Tide will be secure in our vault. You've got nothing to worry about. The Order of the Veiled Cross's mission will be fulfilled."

Elias threw back his head and laughed. "The Order of the Veiled Cross is dead and has been for a century. The Cult of Astaroth took it over and assumed its identity. We knew it was only a matter of time before we found a way to free Umbral Tide. I thought we found it when Mustafa bought the orb, but then Ahmed killed the fool before he could turn it over to me. Imagine my delight when I learned that the one who killed him had showed up to finish the job. Now, the seal and prison."

Black lightning lanced out from the Staff of Law. The bolt smashed through Elias's chest. Instead of collapsing, his body melted into a flesh-colored sludge.

Taking that as a signal, every gun opened up on them. Bullets pinged off their shield, ricocheting all over the place but doing no one any damage.

Daisuke gathered power and shaped it into a wave of

entropy. The black energy rolled out, doing the men no harm but reducing their weapons to scrap metal. With the courtyard silent once more both sides eyed each other as if uncertain what to do next.

Never one to think overly long about things, Daisuke took his pistol out of his bag and marched forward. One by one he blasted the cultists. Some died instantly while others collapsed, writhing in pain. As long as they were out of the fight, Daisuke didn't care one way or the other.

Ruq dove in, eager to join the slaughter. His stinger proved as effective as the bullets. Some of the men tried to flee and Daisuke shot them in the back without mercy. Now that he knew they were Astaroth cultists, he had no compunction about wiping them out.

Halfway through the job he ran out of cartridges and ejected the magazine. Two of the survivors charged him, unarmed.

A hard swing of the staff crushed the first one's head. The second went down a moment later with Ruq's stinger in the side of his neck.

Daisuke finished reloading and got back to work. Killing unarmed men brought him neither pleasure nor satisfaction. It was a mechanical process; pull the trigger, watch them fall, move on to the next one. The whole thing took about ten minutes, then only he and Anatoly remained standing in the courtyard surrounded by the dead.

"What was the point of that?" Anatoly asked. "Did they simply hope to get lucky?"

"They worship the Lord of the Undead, clearly sanity isn't an issue for them. Perhaps they were stupid enough to think we'd just stand there until they wore down our shield." Daisuke put the pistol away and sighed. "It's a shame Elias turned out to be a homunculus. Now we need to hunt him down along with Umbral Tide. Hopefully we've at least dealt with the bulk of their soldiers."

"I'm not counting on it," Anatoly said.

"Me either. I—" He sensed power stir a moment before Jinx emerged from the keep's shadow.

She ran over and hugged him. "The boss sent me to warn you about them, but I was too late. When the fight started I was so worried. Are you okay?"

"Fine, as you can see."

"I am unharmed as well," Anatoly added for good measure.

Daisuke grinned at the dry comment. "Jinx, this is Anatoly, a fellow Circle agent. What was the message?"

Jinx offered a smile and nod to Anatoly then said, "According to Donny, they injected themselves with powdered black iron which let them mimic a powerful demonic aura. That's what blocked your spells. It also kills them in about half a year."

"I sensed nothing," Anatoly said.

"Me either." Daisuke walked over to the nearest body and got busy stripping it. A complex magic circle covered the guy's chest. Daisuke had never seen one like it before. "I bet this does something."

He took out his phone and snapped a couple pictures. Three other bodies had the same circle tattooed on their chests. He didn't bother checking the rest.

"The boss said you should contact her as soon as possible," Jinx said.

"I will, but first let's get back to the oasis. I've had enough of this castle."

Angelique paced in her office. Her gaze kept darting to her phone, willing it to ring. Unfortunately, it just sat there on the corner of her desk, silently mocking her. Plenty of time had passed for Jinx to reach Egypt. In fact, via the shadow paths, she should've been there seconds after leaving Istanbul. That being the case, what was the bloody hold-up? She'd made a point of stressing the importance of the message.

She sat at her desk and started drumming her fingers on the top. Something had to have gone wrong, but she couldn't imagine what. That wasn't true. She could easily imagine any number of things going wrong. Jinx might've arrived too late. The magicproof killers might've been more than Daisuke and Anatoly could handle. The parade of horrible possibilities ended when her phone finally rang.

She snatched it up before the first ring finished. "Daisuke?"

"Sorry for the delay, boss." His voice came through clearly despite the distance. "We had to deal with some complications."

The tension drained from her shoulders. He was okay. That was the main thing. "What happened?"

"Elias and his boys turned up and thought they could kill us with guns. Turns out they were mistaken. I, on the other hand, had no trouble killing them with a gun. Apparently the Cult of Astaroth has basically taken over the Order of the Veiled Cross. They've been wearing it like a skin suit for a century or so."

Her grip tightened on the phone. "That explains the black iron they're using. Did you secure the demon?"

"No. Umbral Tide escaped, though the holy energy did a number on it. I do have the prison and seal, so hunting it down shouldn't be a huge problem. Elias is still in the wind, but we did eliminate about twenty of their cultists."

"Focus on the demon. Elias will keep until it's secure."

"My very plan, boss. But if Elias and the demon both serve the same master, it strikes me as a solid possibility that I'll find them together."

"Is he strong enough for his presence to be an issue?" Angelique asked. "From what you've said I gathered he was just an ordinary human."

"That's what I thought too, but now I'm pretty sure I've been talking to a homunculus this whole time. Assuming that's the case, I have no idea how strong or weak he might be."

"That's not very encouraging. Anyone sufficiently skilled at alchemy to create a humanoid homunculus realistic enough to pose as a professor can't be underestimated. Be careful, both of you."

"We will be," Daisuke said. "Is it cool if Jinx sticks around? A little extra firepower wouldn't hurt and she's game."

"That's fine. I wasn't planning to order her back in any case."

"Great. Was there anything else?"

"No. Keep me informed."

"I will. Also, after we hang up, I'm going to text you a couple images. They're spell circles I found on the dead killers' bodies. I'm thinking they're the reason we couldn't sense their corruption. No idea if it's important, but any info would be welcome."

"I'll get Donny on it. Send them through." Angelique

disconnected and a moment later a text with two images attached appeared in her phone.

She studied the spell circles for a moment but was forced to admit she'd never seen anything like them. It took a moment to print hard copies then she stood and took a step toward the door.

The phone rang again, Helena this time. As soon as she picked it up, Helena said, "Let me go to Cairo, boss. I can be there as backup."

"You're in no shape for that. After back-to-back missions I doubt you're close to fifty percent much less one hundred. Daisuke, Jinx, and Anatoly can handle this one."

"Jinx has done as much as I have over the last few days."

"Jinx isn't human and doesn't have the same weaknesses. We discovered that already. You're not going to change my mind. Get home and recover. When the next crisis pops up, and we all know it will, you need to be ready."

"Fine, but I hate feeling useless."

"How do you think I feel? I'm constantly stuck in the office coordinating things, but unable to really affect the outcomes of our missions. It's horribly frustrating. But we all have our parts to play. Right now mine is to take a new bit of magical trivia to Donny for research. See you tomorrow."

Angelique scrubbed a hand across her face. Sometimes she felt more like a scolding mother than an employer. A little smile quirked her lips. She wouldn't have it any other way.

CHAPTER SEVENTEEN

Daisuke hung up after his quick update to the boss and texted her the pictures he took. Hopefully she, or more likely Donny, would be able to figure out what the spell circles meant. Either way it was out of Daisuke's hands. He couldn't exactly do research in the middle of the desert.

The palms' shadows were getting a little long for comfort, and the idea of letting Umbral Tide get any further away and doing heaven only knew what damage didn't sit well with him.

"Unless you guys really think we shouldn't, I'm going to see if I can track down the demon."

"We have about three hours of daylight," Anatoly said. "I would not waste it."

"The sooner we find it the better," Jinx said.

"Great. You two break camp and I'll see what I can find." Daisuke hadn't thought they'd argue, but the confirmation that they were on the same page encouraged him.

He stood and held the Staff of Law straight out from his

body and focused on Umbral Tide's seal. He'd done this before, but tracking a demon felt different than tracking a human. The corruption made it tricky and this particular demon's lack of a physical form didn't help.

Ether flowed through the seal and Daisuke shaped it into a seeking spell. He turned a slow circle, getting no response after the first revolution. On the second he got a faint tug generally west. Please, please, please don't let the evil thing be headed for a big city. He relaxed a fraction when, on the third rotation, the pull strengthened toward the southwest. It wasn't that far away either, less than a hundred miles. That meant it hadn't left the Sinai.

Maybe it planned to restore itself by killing terrorists. Daisuke didn't object to that as long as it didn't regain too much power.

"I got it. Southwest and it doesn't seem to be moving."

"What's southwest of here?" Jinx asked.

"Beats me," Daisuke said. "Given the distance it's got to still be in the Sinai. Let's go see."

They piled into the truck with Anatoly behind the wheel. Three of them in the cab made a tight fit. Jinx had to practically sit on his lap and Daisuke was okay with that too.

They set out across the rough desert terrain, bouncing and rattling as they followed the tug of the seeking spell, with Ruq flying ahead to scout the way. At this speed they'd need at least a couple hours to get wherever the demon waited.

To kill time Daisuke asked, "How did it go in Istanbul?"

"Pretty well," Jinx said. "The death glider wasn't very strong, but it was so fast we had trouble hitting it."

She gave them a rundown of everything that happened and Daisuke couldn't help grinning when she got to the part where Helena told off the smuggler captain. He would've paid good money to have seen their reaction when Jinx conjured her shadows.

"Anyway, it ended alright, though I felt bad for the sailors we couldn't rescue."

"Yeah, it's always tough when you leave loose ends flapping in the wind," Daisuke said. "But sometimes that's the job. You can't save everyone. Our job is to focus on those things only we can do. I've told Helena that on several occasions but I'm not sure she believes it yet."

"She told me if you'd been there, you'd have killed Captain Demir and dumped his body in the sea."

Daisuke rolled his eyes. "I'm not nearly as bloodthirsty as she likes to pretend."

"You shot twenty guys without blinking an hour ago," Anatoly said.

"Magicproof demon cultists who tried to shoot us first. Totally justified."

They chatted about random stuff until the seeking spell indicated they were only a few miles out.

I see lights.

Anyone they encountered out here was bound to be trouble. "Ruq spotted something ahead of us and the spell indicates Umbral Tide is only a couple miles away. Slow down. We don't want to run into anything unpleasant."

Anatoly slowed to ten miles an hour and they crept on. Daisuke pulled out his phone and opened the browser. Or he tried to. They had no signal out here. So much for trying to figure out where they were.

Looks like a ruin of some sort. It's surrounded by big flaming braziers.

Another ruin, terrific. Not that their destination surprised Daisuke. There wasn't much civilization out here.

Ten minutes later the ruin came into view. Tumbled, broken columns, shattered walls, and scattered rubble littered the area. All very standard stuff. But the lights made it clear someone had moved in and the demon's presence suggested they harbored evil intentions.

"Let's park and go the rest of the way on foot," Daisuke said.

Anatoly guided the truck behind a tall dune that would shield it, at least somewhat, from view. The trio climbed out of the cab and Daisuke passed the pistol to Anatoly. Between the staff and Umbral Tide's prison, Daisuke didn't have enough hands for everything.

They stalked across the sand, quiet as shadows. Approaching with the setting sun in their faces didn't make it any easier to see, and Daisuke squinted against the glare. He could just make out figures, their dark robes fluttering in the evening breeze, moving around the perimeter of the ruin.

One of them paused by a brazier and raised a set of binoculars.

"Down." Daisuke dropped to the sand and the others joined him a second later.

They stayed stock-still until the guard resumed his patrol. Daisuke blew out a breath. That had been too close. What could they be looking for out here? If you looked up the middle of nowhere in the dictionary you'd find a picture of this place.

The answer came to him a moment later. The guards were watching for them. And only Elias could've warned them to expect Daisuke and his companions. Just as Daisuke feared, the demon had come to join its fellow servant of Astaroth. On the plus side, they wouldn't have to go searching for Elias later.

They continued surveilling the ruin for fifteen minutes. One of the guards would scan the horizon at regular intervals. They were definitely on full alert.

"I count eight on patrol," Anatoly said.

"Yeah, not too many, but if they're magicproof taking them out quietly is going to be an issue."

"Do we want to take them out quietly?" Jinx asked.

"What do you mean?" Daisuke asked.

"Well, if we raise a big ruckus, the demon might come out, then you can capture it."

"That's not a terrible idea, but if we do that and it doesn't attack, we'll have alerted Elias and Umbral Tide to our presence. It's a risk either way." Daisuke glanced at Anatoly. "What do you think?"

Anatoly shook his head. "You're the one who has to capture it. Whatever you decide is good with me."

That wasn't terribly helpful. "I doubt their demonic aura would allow them to see through an illusion. Ruq, turn invisible and fly in front of one of them. Let me know if they react."

If I get shot I want extra ice cream. Bullets sting.

Daisuke felt Ruq dive. When a minute passed without any gunfire he felt confident the guards couldn't see invisible things. That was good to know. They could sneak in close and take them out one by one.

He explained his plan to the others and Jinx shook her head. "I don't think I can do that. I've never killed anyone up close. I'm afraid I'll hesitate."

Daisuke patted her arm. "That's okay. Anatoly, Ruq and I

will handle it. You can hang on to the prison, stay on the shadow paths, and keep an eye out. Make sure nothing comes out of the ruin and takes us by surprise."

She offered a weak smile. "Thanks."

Luckily for Daisuke he still had one of the Veiled Cross daggers in his bag. He offered it to Anatoly. Daisuke would have to make do with the staff. Not that crushing an unaware person's skull would be any less effective than cutting their throat.

"Ready?" Daisuke asked.

Anatoly nodded and faded out of sight until only his outline remained visible to Daisuke's magical vision. Daisuke cast his own invisibility spell a moment later and hurried toward the ruins. He could sense Ruq's eagerness. His familiar had gotten to sting a bunch of people to death on this job and he was having a ball. Probably best not to think too much about that.

Daisuke crept forward, keeping his footsteps light on the sand. The first guard stood by a brazier, scanning the horizon with his binoculars. Daisuke gripped the Staff of Law with both hands and swung it in an overhead arc. The guard's skull caved in with a wet crunch and he crumpled without a sound.

A little ways further on, Anatoly's outline slipped behind another guard. A flash of steel and the man dropped, clutching his throat. Blood sprayed between his fingers as he thrashed in the sand.

Two down, six to go.

Ruq swooped and stung the next guard in the neck. The man's muscles locked up as the venom took hold. He toppled face-first into the sand, dead before he hit the ground.

The remaining guards continued their patrol, oblivious to

their dwindling numbers. Daisuke circled wide around a broken column and came up behind his next target. A hard thrust to the back of his skull was followed by another crunch and another body in the sand.

Anatoly took care of two more in quick succession, his dagger finding vital spots with surgical precision. The Russian showed no hesitation, just quick, efficient kills. This was one of the rare times he was glad not to have Helena as his partner on a mission.

The last two guards stood close together, chatting in low voices. Daisuke gestured to Anatoly and held up three fingers. They moved in from opposite sides. He silently counted to three then they struck in unison.

And just like that the coast was clear. No alarm went up and nothing came boiling out of the ruins. So far so good.

Daisuke released his invisibility spell and knelt beside his final victim. He yanked the man's robe aside and sure enough he had one of the spell circles tattooed on his chest.

Ruq landed on his shoulder. "All clear inside. There's an entrance leading underground with more braziers lighting up a long hallway."

Of course they had to go underground again. Heaven forbid they could do this on the surface.

"Jinx," Daisuke whispered.

She appeared silently from a nearby shadow. "There's a barrier stopping me from entering the ruin via the shadow paths. As far as I can tell, there's nothing else dangerous out here."

Looked like nothing remained to do but go in and see what they found waiting for them.

Elias sensed the first of his guards die. He knew who had to be out there: the youthful wizard who destroyed his homunculus, Daisuke Kugo, and his companion. They'd arrived sooner than he expected. Disappointing but hardly a surprise. Three more guards died in quick succession. Once they finished with those outside, the pests would certainly be headed his way.

The Cult of Astaroth had spent nearly a century fortifying Serabit el-Khadim to serve as their base in the area. The former mine and ancient temple dedicated to some imagined god of gemstones made an ideal headquarters for the cult. Its remote location along with the violent reputation of the locals served to keep troublesome visitors away.

He felt confident that, no matter how strong the wizards might be, they wouldn't find the path down an easy one. Nevertheless, he couldn't dawdle. Should they arrive before he completed his transformation, Elias had no confidence in his ability to defeat them.

Elias left his alchemy lab and descended the worn stone steps into the temple's heart. Hieroglyphs older than human civilization decorated the walls, the fanged skull of Astaroth interspersed among them. He'd inscribed even smaller spell circles to increase the ambient corruption.

The air grew thicker with each step, the metallic tang of blood and copper mixing with the ancient evil which permeated every surface. He took a deep breath, savoring the delicious miasma. Hopefully the demon would find it an agreeable atmosphere, though even if it did, Elias doubted that would be enough to put it in a good mood. Assuming you could put a demon in a good mood.

The final chamber opened before him, a vast circular space hewn from living rock. Dozens of brass braziers lined the room, their flames casting writhing shadows across the walls and floor. At the chamber's center, a complex spell circle stretched thirty feet in diameter, its lines carved deep and filled with gold that pulsed with a sickly green light.

Stone pillars rose to the vaulted ceiling, each wrapped in chains of Hell-forged black iron that served as anchors for the spell. The links rattled with each of Umbral Tide's attempts to break free.

Inside the circle, Umbral Tide thrashed against its bonds. The demon's dark form rippled like oil on water as it formed a variety of weapons to slam against the invisible walls. The cult had been working since they settled here to make the spell circle inescapable. Elias felt confident even a greater demon would have no hope of freeing itself.

He was wagering his life on it.

"The wizard is coming," Elias said. "I'm not strong enough to defeat him on my own. You have two choices. Fuse with me or return to your bronze prison."

"Convenient for you, Priest," the demon said. "Your magic dragged me here and bound me like a lamb for the slaughter and unless I give you what you want, I have no options. Had you done this to someone else, I would've been impressed."

"What will you do?" Elias asked.

"I'm tempted to refuse just to let you die for the insult of daring to capture me. I spent over a thousand years in that prison then another thousand trapped in a different sort of prison. Whatever I might think of you, I will not go back in."

"Do you agree to the binding ritual?"

"Yes."

Elias smiled. He'd been waiting for this moment ever since he'd learned of Umbral Tide's existence from his former master. Lord Astaroth had to be watching over him. Nothing else could explain his good fortune.

He walked up to the edge of the spell circle and said in Infernal, "Let darkness and flesh become one."

A second, smaller spell circle appeared under his feet before expanding to touch the first. The moment they made contact, they combined into a single spell. Cold and power unlike anything Elias had ever dreamed of flowed into him.

He lost all awareness as the spell turned him into something far greater than a man.

CHAPTER EIGHTEEN

After Anatoly helped himself to one of the guards' machine guns, Daisuke led the way to the passage Ruq found. The narrow tunnel descended at a steep angle, the ancient limestone worn smooth by centuries of use. Bronze braziers lined the walls, their flames dancing with an unnatural green tinge that cast wavering shadows across defaced hieroglyphs. Demonic symbols mingled with the ancient designs made a bizarre combination.

The braziers' smoke carried a rotten smell that reminded Daisuke of a week-old corpse. An appropriate perfume for a temple of Astaroth. A simple detection spell confirmed that, while unpleasant, the stench had no harmful effects.

Other than the dimensional barrier Jinx mentioned, he couldn't sense any active magic. That seemed odd, as did the lack of any obvious guardians. From the surface, the ruin didn't look that big, but he had no doubt the dungeon would prove depressingly large.

They advanced, slow and steady, with Daisuke in the lead, followed by Jinx, and Anatoly bringing up the rear. Ruq flew around near the ceiling. The imp was surprisingly sensitive to certain sorts of magic. Hopefully, if Elias left them a nasty surprise, Ruq would spot it first.

"How deep do you think this goes?" Jinx asked once they'd descended at least fifty yards.

Daisuke shook his head. "No idea, but I'm sure it'll be deeper than we want to go. On the plus side, I assumed we'd be fighting our way through cultists, demons, and every other flavor of nasty Elias could throw at us. Sometimes it's good to be wrong."

The words had barely left his mouth before he spotted four sets of glowing red eyes farther down the tunnel. He could just make out shadowy figures in the meager light before they lunged forward, more flying than running, toward Daisuke and his companions.

Jinx hurled black flames that burned one of the demons away while Anatoly took out a second with a blast of focused ether shaped like a fist. That left the central pair for Daisuke, and he wiped them out with a burst of black lightning.

They stayed ready for a few more seconds but nothing else tried to kill them.

As they resumed walking Anatoly said, "I didn't expect wraiths."

"I didn't really think about it," Daisuke said. "Compared to what we might've run into, wraiths aren't so bad."

They descended another fifty or so yards before the passage leveled out and widened into a proper chamber. The corruption grew thicker every moment and Daisuke sensed the source at the bottom of the nearby steps. Umbral Tide had to be down there. A second door led to an unknown room.

Daisuke debated for only a second before moving toward

the stairs. Hopefully nothing would come up behind them, but either way he didn't dare waste the time it would take to search.

Halfway down the steps, the corruption grew so thick it forced Daisuke to conjure an extra layer of protection. He glanced at Anatoly and found a similar shield in place around him. Jinx hadn't complained and he assumed her half-demon nature offered some resistance.

The landing at the bottom of the stairs opened into a vast circular cavern, its walls polished to a mirror sheen that reflected sickly green light from dozens of bronze braziers. Corruption hung like an oily mist in the air, making Daisuke's eyes water. Ancient limestone columns ringed the room, each hung with chains of black iron.

In the center, a massive magic circle stretched thirty feet across the floor. Gold-inlaid runes made intricate patterns through the stone, creating nested rings of arcane symbols. The ethereal waves nearly blinded Daisuke's magical vision.

He blinked a few times to clear his watering eyes. Elias stood at the circle's heart, arms raised as dark energy coursed through his body. The professor's skin had taken on a gray cast, and his features were sunken like a century-dead corpse. All around him writhed a mass of pure darkness, Umbral Tide in all its dubious glory. Tendrils of shadow reached out from the demon's core, piercing Elias in a dozen places.

The air crackled as demon and man merged.

Daisuke hurled black lightning at the spell circle, trying in vain to halt the ritual. His spell hit a barrier an inch from impact. Hellfire, elemental energy of all sorts, even holy flames met the same fate. Try as he might, Daisuke couldn't get through.

A sudden wind howled through the chamber.

"Any suggestions?" Daisuke had to shout to be heard over the gale.

His companions could only shake their heads. Anatoly looked on the verge of passing out and pain twisted Jinx's face. If they couldn't get through, then they had to wait and hopefully strike Elias down as soon as he completed the transformation.

Daisuke grabbed each of his companions by the arm and tugged them back toward the stairs. The pressure, while still present, grew bearable this far from the spell circle.

"What's he turning into?" Jinx asked.

"Nothing good," Daisuke said. "I suspect Elias is becoming what the Devil Man aspired to be, an amalgam of demon and human. Hopefully we did enough damage to Umbral Tide that he won't be unstoppable."

"What are the odds of that?" Anatoly asked.

Daisuke's smile held no humor. "For both our sakes and those of Egypt, we'd best hope they're decent."

"Something's happening," Jinx said.

Daisuke turned his full focus on the spell circle. Umbral Tide's darkness had largely vanished. Elias had grown a foot taller and his body had the mass of an ogre, though one with black veins pulsing with corruption just under the surface of his skin. His face still looked human, but nothing else did.

Cracks ran through the spell circle and the air seemed to vibrate. Darkness exploded outwards.

Daisuke hastily conjured a shield.

And lucky for them he did. A wave of corruption denser than anything he'd ever encountered washed over it. Cracks appeared in his shield here and there and for a moment he feared it wouldn't hold. Before it could shatter, Anatoly added his own shield, reinforcing the barrier. Through the silent explosion, Daisuke could feel the darkness screaming in his soul.

Moment by moment the energy faded until he could see Elias standing in the center of the chamber, a cloak of pure darkness made of wisps of Umbral Tide's essence swirling around him.

As soon as he had a clear line of sight, Daisuke hurled a bolt of black lightning.

Elias held out a contemptuous hand and deflected it into the ceiling. That had been one of Daisuke's stronger spells and it didn't so much as singe Elias's palm.

"I'm impressed the three of you survived the end of my spell." Elias's voice was deeper and darker than before, but still clearly him. "Killing you will be the perfect way to test my new powers."

A desperate plan popped into Daisuke's head. "Umbral Tide! By my blood and the power of the staff you are bound. I command you to kneel!"

Elias snarled and thrashed as his legs buckled. The demon part of him wanted to obey, Daisuke could feel it through his connection to the Staff of Law, but the human part refused to give in.

With a roar of rage, pain, or some combination of the two, Elias leapt, crashed through the ceiling, and blasted through layers of dirt and stone until he reached the sky and vanished.

Daisuke blew out a breath and relaxed. That had been the second-best result he could've hoped for. They'd survived for now, but how they were going to defeat the combined man and demon, Daisuke had no idea.

CHAPTER NINETEEN

Angelique flipped to the second page of Donny's report. The spell circle was a good deal more complex than they'd first thought. In addition to hiding the demonic corruption, it had a secondary purpose that Donny had yet to isolate. Something specific to Astaroth, but beyond that he wasn't sure.

You'd think after all these years she'd be used to uncertainty, but familiarity didn't help in the slightest. She needed to know if any ongoing threat lingered or if killing the men ended the danger.

She rubbed her eyes and wished, not for the first time, that she could sleep, even for only a couple of hours, so she didn't have to think. But her angelic blood didn't allow that. Sometimes she thought it a curse and others, a blessing. Right now she was definitively leaning toward the former.

Her phone rang and she jumped. Midnight had come and gone not long ago. Why would Daisuke call at this hour? Somehow she doubted he had good news.

"Daisuke?"

"We've got serious trouble, boss. Elias found a way to merge with Umbral Tide. He slapped away a bolt of black lightning like it was nothing. On the upside, I can sort of command him with the staff. Unfortunately he flew off before I could find out if his demon side would submit or his human side resist."

Heaven's mercy, that was about the worst news she could've imagined. "Where's Elias now?"

"According to the tracking spell, headed northwest. Given his bearing I'd say he's going to Cairo. To do what has me considerably worried."

"As well it should. I'll contact my agents in the city and see what's going on. Get there as fast as you can."

"Will do, boss. The thing is, I'm not at all sure what we can accomplish when we arrive. The only way we can beat him is to separate the demon from the man and I haven't the least idea how to go about doing so. Crimson Haze would melt my eyes before I could come close to burning away Umbral Tide. If you have any suggestions, I'm all ears."

"I wish I did. Just do the best you can and we'll see what we can figure out on this end. Even if you can't beat him, you might be able to disrupt whatever he has planned in the city. Be creative."

"Right, creative. Thanks, boss. I'll be in touch."

Daisuke hung up and she sighed. How in the world were they going to separate Professor Elias from Umbral Tide? And if they couldn't, how were they going to beat a man with the power of a greater demon?

Elias soared through the night sky, the desert wind whipping at his clothes. Raw power unlike anything he'd ever imagined coursed through him, filling him to bursting with demonic energy. His new body left something to be desired in terms of appearance. There was nothing subtle about a nearly eight-foot-tall, gray-skinned ogre after all. Not that he needed to be subtle, not with his new, unstoppable power.

At least he'd thought it was unstoppable. The memory of Daisuke daring to give him a command—him! likely the most powerful being in the world or at a minimum in Africa —made Elias's blood boil. The magic had struck him like a physical blow, nearly bringing him to his knees. For a brief, terrifying moment, he'd felt an overwhelming urge to submit. Only once he'd put some distance between himself and the wizard did that feeling fade.

He pushed himself faster, his shadowy wings spreading wider as he rushed to reach his hidden lair. From there he could begin the next phase of his plan.

The lights of Cairo appeared on the horizon. He slowed then glided down to land on the roof of the main building on the university campus. The secret of what he'd built underneath remained a secret known only to the High Warden of the sect. Well, technically what his predecessors had built. If the ruin was their first temple, the one under the university was the second and most convenient.

No one saw him rip the roof-access door off its hinges then squeeze his too-broad shoulders through the frame. Despite the tight fit he was soon stomping down the stairs three at a time. This stairway descended all the way to the basement and he didn't stop until he reached it.

A second door went flying at his tug and Elias grimaced.

He had to get that under control before he damaged something important. His workshop held some vital, and more importantly delicate, equipment. Replacing it would be a nuisance.

He followed a silent, empty hallway to a storeroom packed with cleaning supplies. An application of dark power triggered the hidden door in the back wall, which swung open to reveal another set of steps down to the temple.

As soon as he got clear, Elias sealed the entrance behind him. The absolute darkness proved no issue for his demon-enhanced eyes and after a short walk he reached his workshop just off the chapel. Two tables covered with alchemy supplies took up much of the space while two glass cylinders big enough for a normal human to fit inside sat against the rear wall. Finally, a small bookcase held his reference books. Everything remained exactly as he'd left it.

"So, what happened?" Elias asked.

What do you mean?

"I mean, how did that boy, that pathetic, mortal youth, somehow have the power to command me? I should be unstoppable now that I have your power, yet I think if I hadn't fled when I did, I might well have submitted to him. How is that possible?"

He has Solomon the Wise's staff and my seal. Those, combined with the proper spells, grant him the power to compel me. And worse, should he find some way to separate us, he will be able to imprison me once more.

"Unacceptable. This is a serious impediment to claiming the world for Lord Astaroth. How do we overcome it?"

Kill him.

Elias waited but that was the sum of the demon's brilliant advice. Kill the boy. How was he supposed to do that when

Daisuke could simply command him to surrender? He ground his teeth then forced himself to relax. His anger came far more quickly since his transformation. He'd have to be careful of that. Elias's strengths up to now had been cleverness and subtlety. He couldn't let his newfound might blind him.

If he couldn't kill Daisuke himself, perhaps his servants would have better luck.

He moved to the center of the room and sent invisible tendrils of power out into the city. All the men who had been slain in his service would rise once more. He sent demonic energy into the spell circles he'd drawn on their chests and activated their secondary function.

The moment he sensed newborn thralls begin to shift, he imprinted a simple command onto their crude minds.

Kill everyone.

Eagerness met his command. Nothing in the city could stop his creations and the chaos would be certain to draw Daisuke's attention. Once the thralls killed him, Elias would be free to emerge and begin the important business of turning this city into a tomb worthy of Astaroth.

CHAPTER TWENTY

Daisuke hung up and pocketed his phone. The boss not knowing how to separate Elias and Umbral Tide didn't surprise him. Nobody kept that sort of information just rattling around in the back of their head.

"What did she say?" Jinx asked.

"She wants us to go to Cairo and try to keep the damage to a minimum until she can research a way to separate them. I figure you and me shadow walk to the city while Anatoly stays here to try and figure out exactly what Elias did."

"Hmm, I'm not sure I'm crazy about that plan," Anatoly said.

"Do you want to go to Cairo with Jinx and I'll stay here?" Daisuke asked. "Even with the staff, I have no hope of beating him one on one, but if you'd like to try..."

"On second thought, research is fine. There isn't much left of the spell circle down here, but maybe there'll be something upstairs in the room we bypassed."

"Good thinking. Stay in touch with the boss. Maybe she can even convince Donny to get on the line with you."

"I've known Donny longer than you and I've never spoken to him in person, not even on the phone. I think the prospect scares him more than the end of the world."

"Don't underestimate the boss's persuasive abilities. Good luck. Ready, Jinx?"

"As I'll ever be."

They retraced their steps outside, stepped onto the shadow paths, and headed for Cairo. Given the time distortion on the paths, Daisuke figured this would be a good time to plan their strategy, at least to the extent they could.

"Even if we find Elias, we're not going to approach directly. Neither of us could even hurt him, so the risk is all on our end. I want to find his base and interrupt whatever plans he might have. Do you have any ideas we might try?"

Jinx shook her head. "I'm way out of my depth here. My magic is all instinctive. I'm not a trained wizard like you and the others. While I'm happy to help out however I can, when it comes to complex analysis or strategy, I'm useless."

Daisuke took her hand. "You're a lot of things, but never useless, so don't talk about yourself that way, and more importantly don't think about yourself that way. You're an important part of the team."

"Thanks."

A few seconds later they emerged in the same dark alley where he and Anatoly found the information broker's body. The slums, at least, seemed calm for the moment.

"Keep a lookout. I need to cast the seeking spell again."

Jinx nodded and he focused on Umbral Tide's seal. After three turns he still hadn't got so much as a tingle to indicate where the demon might be hiding.

Usually you couldn't force the more subtle magic to work, but he decided to risk sending more ether into the seal. One more spin got him a hit. Then another, and another, and another. All in all, he sensed the demon in ten different places around the city. What the hell did that mean? He hadn't screwed up the spell, so something else must be going on.

He homed in on the nearest one. It felt close, less than a mile. "I've got something. Let's check it out."

He and Jinx set out through the dark city, guided by his tracking spell. Their path brought them to a spot across the street from the local police station. Closer now, Daisuke sensed… three pieces of Umbral Tide. At least he thought they were pieces. He'd never felt something like this when casting a tracking spell.

"How are we going to sneak into a police station to see what's going on?" Jinx asked.

She posed an excellent question. As he considered how to respond, the crack of gunfire rang out. What started as a few shots quickly turned into a full-on gun battle with the firecracker roar of automatic weapons mixing in with the slower-paced pops of pistols.

"Sneaking in suddenly seems like less of an issue," Daisuke said. "Come on."

Daisuke and Jinx burst through the front doors of the police station and into a war zone. Bullets pinged off walls and shattered glass partitions. Officers crouched behind desks and doorways, emptying clip after clip at three naked men who strode through the station while making no effort to take cover.

Black flames writhed across spell circles carved into the men's chests. Their slack, blank faces made it clear they were already dead. In fact, Daisuke had killed them himself not long ago. Or at least ones who looked like them.

The air reeked of burnt flesh and gunpowder while the noise nearly deafened him.

"Those are some of Elias's pet killers," Daisuke said. "Looks like the spell circles have absorbed a fragment of Umbral Tide's power and reanimated them as some kind of thrall."

"Can we stop them?" Jinx asked.

"Good question."

A young-looking officer retreated a little too slowly and one of the thralls grabbed him by the throat before lifting him off the ground. He screamed and squeezed the trigger of his pistol again and again with nothing but the hammer's click to show for it.

Daisuke leveled the Staff of Law and cast Disintegration Blade. The powerful spell sliced off the arm holding the unlucky cop at the elbow. He hit the floor and collapsed.

Two of his fellow officers darted in and dragged him, gasping, a safe distance away.

The creatures weren't completely magicproof at least. Thank heaven for small favors.

He cast again, this time summoning a black disk under their feet. Black lightning arced up into their bodies, destroying flesh and leaving their steaming bodies covered in wounds, but still on their feet.

Jinx followed up with a blast of dark fire.

The nearest thrall shuddered and collapsed, the demonic essence finally burned out of it.

Daisuke narrowed his eyes at the other two and activated Crimson Haze. In their damaged state it didn't take long to finish them off and soon the last thrall hit the floor, leaving his eyes stinging but still clear.

They'd barely finished off the thralls when every cop in

the place spun and pointed their guns at them. The ingratitude annoyed him more than the threat itself. Their weapons had no more hope of hurting Daisuke or Jinx than they did the thralls.

"Who the hell are you two?" one of the older officers asked. His pistol shook and he seemed unaware that the slide was locked open, making it clear he was out of rounds.

"We're the wizards who just saved your life," Daisuke said. "How about you point those guns somewhere else before I decide we made a mistake?"

"Right, right, sorry." The officer waved at the others and lowered his own weapon. "It's not every day a resident of the morgue decides to get back up and try to kill you. Many thanks for the help."

Daisuke nodded. That was more like it. "Where did you find these three?"

"I'm not sure. I'm the desk sergeant. I can look it up if you want."

"Forget it. There are a bunch more of these guys in the city. We need to go deal with them. If you really want to help, you can contact every other station, give them our descriptions, and let them know we're here to help. If any of the people I'm risking my life to save shoot at me, I'm going to be irritated."

"I can do that, no problem. In fact, why don't you take a couple of the boys with you. That'll clear things up in a hurry."

From the looks on the other officers' faces, none of them planned to volunteer for that job. Not that they were going to have to. "No, thanks. Bringing a non-wizard along would only slow us down and add potential victims in need of protection. Making the call will be enough."

"As you wish. Best of luck to you."

"I'll take all I can get," Daisuke said. "Let's go."

He led Jinx outside and renewed the tracking spell. He sensed the next group close to the center of the city, a heavily populated area. If they didn't get there quickly, it was going to be a slaughter.

CHAPTER TWENTY-ONE

Anatoly finished studying what remained of the shattered spell circle, but could make nothing of it. He didn't even recognize most of the runes Elias had used. Despite feeling totally out of his depth with this job, he knew he was the best one to handle it. While far from a poor fighter, he couldn't hold a candle to Daisuke or Jinx. Hopefully he could find something useful upstairs.

He stomped up the steps. With everyone dead he saw no point in sneaking around. At the top, he crossed the circular chamber to the closed door they'd bypassed earlier. A simple detection spell confirmed a lack of defensive wards. He jiggled the handle then gave it a shove. It opened easily and he stepped inside.

Anatoly's nose wrinkled at the sharp tang of ozone mixed with incense and rotting flesh. He conjured a light and grimaced at the fifty-foot-square windowless chamber which served as Elias's workshop. Benches lined both walls, their surfaces scarred and stained dark brown. Glass containers filled with preserved organs floated in murky liquid. A half-dissected corpse lay spread across one table. Its leathery hide had been peeled back to expose its guts. Anatoly had no idea what the thing used to be beyond not human.

Leaving the unpleasant biology experiment behind, he focused on a brass pedestal near the right rear wall. A black, leather-bound tome rested on it. Given its prominence, he had high hopes that he might find something useful inside.

Ignoring everything else, he strode over to the pedestal. Once more he checked for magical protections and once more he came up empty. Elias must've had great faith in his followers, a rare thing among demon worshippers. Not that he planned to complain. The lack of wards made his life much easier.

He opened the book to page one and frowned. The author had written it in Infernal. Hardly a surprise given the setting. All Circle agents were reasonably fluent in the demon tongue, it was a necessity given their work, so he started reading.

His theory about the book's importance proved correct. He'd stumbled onto Elias's working journal. He scanned entries detailing Elias's early days in the cult, his failures when it came to priestly magic, his punishments for those failures, and his eventual success with alchemy and spell circles.

Here we go. The first mention of Umbral Tide and his plan to merge his body with the demon's, thus gaining control of its power.

A distant noise caught his attention. Sounded like something scraping. He focused his awareness and sensed new sources of corruption. Still a safe distance away, but close enough to worry him.

He got out his phone and dialed the boss.

She must've been waiting as the second ring had barely started when she said, "Anatoly, what news?"

"I found Elias's journal. It covers his plans for merging with Umbral Tide. There are a lot of technical details that go way over my head."

"Have Jinx or Daisuke bring that book here at once."

"They've already left for Cairo."

"Then call them back. This is too important for any delay."

The scraping outside was getting louder. He lifted his rifle and eased over to the door. Nothing was visible outside, but something was definitely headed his way.

"Anatoly? Are you still there?"

"Yes, boss. I'll call them."

"Good. If you find anything else, let me know."

She disconnected and he tapped Daisuke's number. It rang until his voicemail answered. He'd never ignore Anatoly's call, not now. Something had to be going on.

Anatoly hung up and sent a text instead. Heaven only knew how long it would take Daisuke to check his voicemail.

With nothing better to do, he returned to the journal and read some more. While he didn't understand the details, it quickly became clear Elias had spent a lot of time preparing for the ritual. The amount of effort he expended was remarkable given the numerous acknowledgements that he had no idea how to gain access to Umbral Tide.

A thud sounded right outside the door. Anatoly tiptoed over and peeked out. Four cultists milled around outside, the spell circles on their chests burning with dark fire. Two of them looked like they'd had their throats cut.

He was considering his next move when his phone rang.

All four of the thralls turned to look at him. Cursing his luck, he shut the door and cast a sealing spell on it. That wouldn't hold off four thralls for long, but it should buy him a little time.

Ten blocks from the police station, Daisuke sensed half a dozen more sources of corruption. They were far weaker than the thralls in the police station, but the magic felt similar.

"What are those?" Jinx asked.

"Let's go see." Daisuke shifted his path to intersect with the slow-moving sources of corruption.

I see them. Looks like either greater zombies or really weak thralls.

A block further on, Daisuke spotted the targets. The creatures were trying to smash their way into an apartment building. Every blow they landed brought the crunch of splintering wood. Luckily for Daisuke, the zombies had gathered in a tight bunch as they fought to be the first to reach the people inside.

He leveled the staff and summoned a black disk under them. Black lightning arced up into the monsters, quickly reducing them to dust. Wisps of darkness, likely the magic which animated them, flew off into the night in the general direction of the city center.

Whatever these new creatures were, they didn't compare to the thralls from the police station. Of course ordinary people, even armed ones, had no hope of defeating them.

Daisuke never thought he'd be missing the magicproof killers, but at least the cops could shoot them.

He was about to reorient himself with the tracking spell when his phone vibrated. A brief text from Anatoly asking for a call back covered the screen.

What could he want after just fifteen minutes? Well, one way to find out.

He hit dial.

After three rings Anatoly said, "Daisuke? I'm in a bit of a situation here. The guys we killed have risen as thralls and they're right outside the door."

"Well, shit. I didn't think Elias's magic would reach that far."

"That's not all. I found Elias's journal and the boss wants it brought to base double quick."

"Okay, hang on. Jinx will be right there. She can take you and the journal back to Zurich."

As soon as he hung up Jinx said, "I can't leave you alone."

"I'll be fine. Plus I have Ruq, so I won't be alone. Get Anatoly and the journal back to base then rejoin me. On the shadow paths it shouldn't take you more than five minutes. I'll see about tracking down the next group of thralls. The black wisps we saw gave me an idea I want to test."

She gave him a searching look. "Okay, but don't do anything crazy until I get back."

"I won't, but hurry."

Jinx stepped into a nearby shadow and vanished. Okay, time to get back to work. He homed in on the next nearest source of corruption, another group of the weak ones. Perfect, that would be his best chance to test his theory.

He jogged after them with Ruq gliding along overhead.

You really think this is going to work?

"I don't know. That's why it's called an experiment. Though I wish I'd thought of it sooner. Demons are just evil spirits after all. If the orb can absorb holy magic, it should be able to absorb corrupt magic. Being able to negate Umbral Tide's magic would certainly come in handy."

It didn't take Daisuke long to hunt down the source of corruption, another group of three weaker thralls. The trio trudged down the street as if not at all certain about their destination. They reminded him of college students after a late night partying. He assumed they had just risen and would soon go on a killing spree. Or try to. He intended to make sure they died again right now.

He leveled the staff and cast a bolt of black lightning. The spell arced from one thrall to the next, burning holes through their chests and sending them crashing to the ground.

They'd barely hit the ground when the black wisps came floating out.

Daisuke thrust the Elemental Orb out and willed it to absorb the wisps. They fought, trying to pull away and return to the source.

Snarling, Daisuke moved closer. When only feet separated them, the orb finally won the battle and sucked the wisps up. A tiny little dot of darkness now floated in the center of the orb. While he doubted the minute speck of corruption would be of any use in a fight, at least it hadn't returned to the demon. He'd take that trade any day.

Now he needed to find the stronger thralls, which were, he assumed, the source of the weak ones.

CHAPTER TWENTY-TWO

Jinx hurried down the shadow paths. She wanted to finish up with Anatoly and get back to help Daisuke as quickly as possible. Leaving him alone in Cairo—she didn't really count Ruq—sat wrong with her. Still, Jinx knew what she had to do if they were going to defeat Elias and Umbral Tide, so she resolved to focus on her task and trust that he'd be okay when she caught up.

When she sensed her destination ahead, Jinx slowed from a run to a walk. Traveling on the paths was strange. If you'd asked her to explain how she knew where she was or how to get somewhere else, she wouldn't have been able to describe the process. It all came down to feelings.

She sensed something wrong a moment before an impenetrable barrier appeared in front of her. Her jaw dropped. She'd forgotten all about the ward which prevented magical entry. She'd been in such a hurry it just slipped her mind. Of all the idiotic things she might've done, this one was at least not apt to get her killed.

But it would slow her down.

She emerged from the shadow paths at the tunnel entrance. No thralls or other visible dangers guarded the entrance. Just to be safe she wrapped herself in invisibility before entering.

Jinx jogged along the tunnel, trying her best to balance speed with stealth. The glowing braziers caused her shadow to dance and wave along the walls despite her invisibility spell. She didn't know how smart the thralls were but if they were paying attention at all, they'd be sure to spot her.

Couldn't worry about that now.

She made good time, encountering no obstacles as she hurried deeper into the ruin. At last she paused about twenty yards from the first chamber. Eight corrupt auras pulsed ahead. She recognized the thralls at once. They felt exactly the same as the ones in Cairo. Dull thuds filled the air. At least the noise would cover her approach.

A few more strides brought her to the chamber entrance. She found the thralls pounding on the door they'd passed earlier when hunting Elias. Anatoly's life force was behind the door, strong and steady. The way the thralls were hammering away didn't fill her with optimism that he'd stay healthy for much longer.

Jinx needed to draw them away, but how?

The creatures showed no sign of tiring. Jinx flexed her fingers, dark fire crackling between them. She couldn't take them on her own, but maybe she could lure them away from Anatoly. If he could just get outside the barrier, Jinx would be free to grab him and escape.

If the thralls split up she'd be in trouble, but given her lack of other options, she canceled her invisibility and shouted, "Hey! Over here!"

Eight sets of burning eyes turned to stare at her.

Well, she'd gotten their attention at least. That was a start.

The thralls wavered, seeming uncertain what to do. Maybe she could give them a bit of encouragement.

A blast of dark fire burned the face off the nearest thrall. It roared and made a horrible expression. As if taking that as a signal, the group charged her.

Jinx turned and ran back the way she'd come, the thralls right on her heels. The cursed things ran far faster than they had any right to. It didn't help that Jinx wasn't the speediest person in the world. When you could shadow walk, regular running seemed kind of pointless.

She risked a glance back over her shoulder and found the red eyes far too close for comfort. Hopefully Anatoly wouldn't waste the opening she'd made for him.

The door had splintered enough to allow Anatoly to see bits of flesh through the gaps. He figured he had at best two minutes before it gave way completely. And when that happened, he didn't know what he might do.

That wasn't true. He knew exactly what he was going to do; either get torn limb from limb or end up as another thrall. Neither prospect filled him with excitement. If it came down to it, he knew a spell that would burn out his life force and hopefully take at least a couple of the thralls with him.

"Hey! Over here!" He recognized Jinx's voice.

The thralls stopped pounding. Through the gaps he could see them all looking away, he assumed at Jinx. Did she have a plan? He hoped so.

A blast of dark fire hit one of the thralls in the face. It

roared and all of them ran off after her. It seemed it wasn't his day to die after all. Not at the moment at least.

He waited a minute to make sure none of them planned to come back, then slipped out of the workshop, Elias's journal under his arm. He took a step to follow them up the tunnel then caught himself. Best to take another way out of here.

He hurried down the steps and into the ritual chamber. The tunnel Elias had blasted in the ceiling remained as they left it. Anatoly focused and activated a levitation spell. A disk of ether lifted him up and out of the ruin.

As soon as his feet touched the sand he wobbled and staggered about like a newborn deer. Something about lifting himself with magic really took it out of him. But he didn't have time to waste recovering.

Once his legs felt strong enough to hold him, Anatoly ran, well, power walked, toward the front entrance. He could sense Jinx's life force as well as the thralls' corruption right behind her. They were far too close for comfort.

He rounded a dune and the entrance came into view. He didn't want to get too close, and the dune cast a perfect shadow. When she reached him, they could dive right into it. Anatoly hated the shadow paths, but right now he'd be glad to pay them a visit.

Jinx came running out of the ruin and he shouted, "Over here!"

She looked his way and immediately adjusted her course.

The snarling, savage pack of thralls emerged a few steps behind her.

He silently urged her to run faster. Anatoly debated casting a spell to try and slow the thralls down, but anything he could manage now wouldn't make a dent. No, it was a footrace and he could only cheer her on.

When Jinx reached ten yards out, he braced himself. She wasn't slowing down at all.

Jinx hit him at a full sprint, drove her shoulder into his gut, and hoisted him onto her shoulder. One more stride sent them onto the shadow paths. Her momentum carried them a couple more staggering steps then Jinx stopped.

"Thank you for the rescue."

"Glad to help," she said between gasps. "How did you get out ahead of me?"

"I levitated out the hole Elias made in the ceiling. It seemed like a safer option than potentially drawing the thralls' attention by coming up behind you."

"Yeah, I never even thought about it. I'm so worried about Daisuke my brain is all over the place." Jinx started walking while carrying Anatoly like a sack of potatoes. "I know he doesn't need me worrying, but I can't help it."

"All we can do is our best. Speaking of, am I too heavy for you?"

"I'm stronger than I look. It's the demon blood. Don't worry, we'll be in Zurich soon. I know traveling like this isn't comfortable."

"I thought I'd be getting torn apart by thralls right about now. Your shoulder in my stomach isn't nearly so bad."

She let out a little laugh. "I suppose not. I'll drop you in the alley behind the shop. Will that be okay?"

"Perfectly. I always have my key with me. Plus the boss will sense our arrival and no doubt meet me at the door."

"Great, here we are." She stepped out of a shadow into the familiar alley behind Arcane Books and Trinkets, set him on his feet, and blew out a breath. "I need to get back to Cairo. The sooner you can figure out how to stop Elias, the better."

And then she vanished back into the shadow paths.

Anatoly put her out of his mind and headed for the entrance. He managed three steps before the door opened, revealing the charming form of their employer.

"Do you have it?" He handed her the journal then followed her inside. As they passed her office she said, "I need to take this to Donny. Have a seat and we'll talk in a minute."

"I'll do my best to stay awake, boss." They parted company and he slipped into the office. The guest chairs had never looked more inviting. He settled into the nearest one and, despite his promise, fell into a light doze.

Angelique left a clearly exhausted Anatoly resting and hurried downstairs. She hadn't even taken the time to glance inside the journal. Donny would have a much better chance of figuring something out than she would and the longer it took him to get started, the longer Daisuke and Jinx would have to fight.

She reached his closed door and pounded on it. This wasn't an occasion she could baby his anxiety, not with lives in the balance. "Donny! We've got an emergency. I need you to figure out how to separate a human and a demon. I'm leaving a journal in front of your door. Text me as soon as you have the answer."

The journal settled on the floor with a loud thud. Angelique listened until she heard approaching footsteps then retreated back upstairs. She could do nothing now but have faith he'd figure it out in time.

Back in her office, she found Anatoly, eyes closed and head tilted back, asleep in her guest chair. Part of her wanted to let him sleep, but she needed to know the situation and a firsthand account would be best.

She gave him a light shake and he immediately sat up. "I was only resting my eyes, boss."

Angelique smiled as she sat in her own chair. "It's okay. I know you've been through a lot. After you give me a final report, you can go upstairs and rest in the infirmary. I'd send you home, but right now I want you on standby in case things go completely wrong."

"I'm not sure how much I can tell you since I stayed in the ruin while Daisuke and Jinx went to Cairo." He described both the workshop and how the killers came back to life as thralls. "I had no hope of beating them so I barricaded myself in the workshop and hoped for the best. Jinx's timely arrival was most welcome."

Angelique nodded. "Raising their corpses must've been the spell circle's secondary function. Donny hadn't figured it out before his last report. The dark fire you mentioned makes me think Elias is using Umbral Tide's magic to raise them rather than summoning demon spirits. That should weaken him a fair bit."

She was talking as much to herself as to Anatoly and when she glanced at him, his eyes had nearly closed again. "Go lie down. You did good work. If heaven smiles I won't have to wake you until it's over."

"I like the sound of that, boss. If you'll excuse me." He stood and shuffled off out of her office.

If he was this worn out, she couldn't imagine how Daisuke and Jinx were holding up. Angelique offered a silent prayer that they'd be strong enough to finish the mission.

CHAPTER TWENTY-THREE

Daisuke pressed his back against the wall of an alley and watched four thralls shamble down the empty street toward him. Their movements, fluid and powerful, looked nothing like their weaker brothers'. Black flames danced across the spell circles on their chests. Pity the police hadn't left their clothes on when they put them in the morgue. He enjoyed few things less than looking at naked male demons.

They hadn't noticed him yet so he had a few seconds to plan. He really wanted to find out if he could use the Elemental Orb to pull the corruption out of them directly. That would be incredibly convenient, so of course he doubted it would work. But he had only one way to find out for sure.

The thralls paused, their heads swinging left and right in unison like a pack of hounds. Well, no sense delaying. He deactivated the spell he'd been using to shield his life force. The moment he did, all four thralls turned and stared right at him. The thralls started his way, picking up speed as they got closer.

He leveled the staff and cast an earth magic spell. The ground exploded around the thralls, sending the group plunging into a pit.

Whoever takes care of the streets is going to be pissed at you.

"If this is the worst thing the Cairo Department of Public Works has to deal with, they can consider themselves lucky. I need to focus, so make sure nothing sneaks up on me."

With Ruq on full alert, Daisuke walked over to the edge of the pit. One of the thralls had nearly reached the top already and the others were clambering up as well. Talk about convenient. He took the Elemental Orb from his satchel, pointed it toward the nearest thrall, and willed it to draw the corrupt ether out of its body.

And nothing happened. Focusing with every ounce of mental energy he could muster, he tried to force the orb to obey.

It made no difference.

It seemed that, as long as the energy remained bound to the spell circle, he couldn't absorb it. Disappointing but hardly surprising.

The thrall's head reached the top of the pit and Daisuke kicked it in the face, sending it sprawling back into the hole. He leveled the staff and blasted it with black lightning which arced from thrall to thrall, pouring more power into the spell until he'd reduced them to charred flesh and bone.

This time when he held the orb out, it did its job, sucking up the freed corruption and adding it to the speck already inside.

Daisuke slumped against the wall of a handy building, his breath coming in short gasps. The black lightning spell had taken more out of him than he'd expected. Four thralls shouldn't have been that difficult to destroy.

"Here." Ruq dropped a candy bar in Daisuke's hand.

"Where'd you get this?"

Ruq jerked a tiny thumb over his shoulder. "There's a shop with a full display of them."

Daisuke unwrapped the chocolate and took a bite. The sugar hit his system and he sighed as his strength returned, a little anyways. "Thanks."

When he'd finished his snack Daisuke pushed away from the wall and focused on the tracking spell. He'd gotten better at figuring out which specks of power were the strong thralls and which the weak ones. Fortunately, he sensed nothing save a single group of strong thralls coming from the general direction of the college. And they weren't moving. Seemed like they should be hunting students in the dorm or something.

Oh well, if they weren't moving it would make the job of hunting them down easier.

He turned toward the college.

"If they're not threatening anyone, you should rest longer," Ruq said. "It's not like we know how to deal with Elias or Umbral Tide yet anyways."

Ruq had a point. Considering his current condition, Daisuke doubted he could beat four of the strong thralls. "Grab a couple more of those candy bars. We'll walk slowly and eat as we go."

Ruq didn't need to be told twice. He flew back toward the shop, rubbing his hands. While it might not be as evil as killing, stealing got his demon blood pumping as well.

"Daisuke!" He nearly blasted Jinx when she spoke from out of nowhere. He'd been so distracted he didn't even sense her arrival. When she hugged him it was just about the most pleasant feeling he'd ever experienced.

"Hey. Did you get Anatoly home safe and sound?"

"Yes, but it was a little tricky. I forgot about the teleportation barrier around the ruin and he was trapped by eight thralls. But we managed."

Ruq dropped two more candy bars in his hand and kept one for himself. Daisuke started for the college at a slow walk. Between bites he filled Jinx in on what he'd learned.

When he finished she said, "So every thrall you destroy and absorb its corruption weakens the demon?"

"That's my theory. Whether it amounts to anything, we won't know until we face off with Elias again. But I am optimistic."

Not *really* optimistic, but he kept that to himself.

A little twinge of pain ran through Elias as another group of thralls died. When he claimed Umbral Tide's power as his own, he'd thought his days of feeling pain were over, but apparently not. Even worse, he only had one group of thralls remaining in the city, and instead of working to expand his legion of followers, they were stationed outside the building on guard duty.

He found the whole situation ludicrous. Why couldn't the world just submit to Astaroth's rule and be done with it? They were only delaying the inevitable.

You humans have an annoying habit of refusing to acknowledge when you're beaten. More importantly, did you notice my power didn't return after the last batch of thralls was destroyed?

Elias frowned. He still didn't fully understand the limits

of his new power and the coming and going of such a minute part of it escaped him. "No, was it supposed to?"

Of course it was supposed to. You're not animating the thralls with a summoned demon spirit, you're using fragments of my essence. The first few returned as they were supposed to, but the last two didn't.

"And what does that mean?"

Elias bristled when Umbral Tide's disgust washed over him. *It means someone has found a way to contain my power. The more thralls you make, the weaker we become. Eventually, if we can't reclaim the power, there will be nothing left and we'll be helpless.*

Being helpless didn't interest Elias at all. He'd bonded with Umbral Tide to avoid ever feeling weak again. "I'll summon the thralls we left behind at the ruins. No one wizard has any hope of defeating so many."

It would be wiser to simply relocate to a distant place and start fresh.

"How would that be wiser? The wizard can track us wherever we might run. At least here we have soldiers to fight for us."

As if those insignificant creatures amount to anything compared to my power.

"Enough! I am the master here and we will do things the way I wish them to be done. And you will keep silent unless I ask you a question. Understand?"

He took Umbral Tide's silence as acquiescence. Good. He always found it rather pitiful when someone didn't recognize their betters.

Elias drew on the demon's magic and pulled all the pieces of himself closer. He felt the thralls appear outside his base and he ordered them to kill anyone who approached. Forty of them now protected his hidden temple. No one could fight their way through such a force.

Umbral Tide remained silent, but Elias could feel the demon's doubts echoing in the back of his mind. Let the evil thing doubt. Elias knew what he was doing.

CHAPTER TWENTY-FOUR

Daisuke crumpled the candy wrapper and shoved it in his pocket. The sugar rush helped clear his head, but he still had a long way to go to fully recover. Daisuke considered it a small miracle that they'd avoided a fight for the last half hour. If they could keep avoiding them for another four or five, he'd be in pretty good shape.

He paused at the edge of the university campus. The remaining four thralls hadn't moved since he last checked on them. They were definitely guarding something, probably Elias's hiding place. It would be just like a professor to use the college as his home base. The guy might be smart about some things, but strategy wasn't one of them.

"What now?" Jinx asked.

"Now we need to take a closer look at the situation."

"You mean I need to," Ruq said.

"I'll be looking with you. Besides, the thralls are much less likely to notice a demon approaching than a human. Stick to the rooftops and you'll be fine."

Ruq grumbled but took off toward the gathered source of corruption. It didn't take him long to land on a handy roof looking down at the front door of the main building. Specifically, at the same door Daisuke went through when he first met Elias.

The thralls seemed content to stand there looking around at nothing in particular. The entire campus was dead quiet. You'd think there'd be some kids out and about going to or coming back from a party. He checked his phone. An hour after midnight. He'd snuck out of the dorms later than this as a teenager. It was kind of pitiful.

But convenient for him. Having some random kid walking into a fight would not be ideal.

What now?

"Now you stay there and keep an eye on them while I rest. We'll give them until an hour before dawn. If nothing's happened before then, I'll destroy the thralls and see about digging Elias out of his hole."

"But we still don't know how to separate Elias from Umbral Tide," Jinx said.

"True. But once the sun comes up, we'll have students and faculty all over the place. It'll be a nightmare to try and deal with them once that happens."

As Daisuke searched for a comfortable place to sit down, a sudden surge of corruption came from the vicinity of the thralls.

"What was that?" Jinx asked.

"Let's see."

Daisuke linked his vision with Ruq's just in time to watch a massive spell circle made of black flames appear in front of the building. Out of the darkness emerged humanoid shapes that quickly resolved into more thralls. Dozens of them.

These had to be the cultists he killed at Taba Castle and the ancient ruins. He hadn't thought Elias would be able to bring them here so easily. Hopefully doing so took a huge toll on him.

"Forty of them," Daisuke muttered, when the spell circle finally vanished. "We are in so much trouble."

"Daisuke?" Jinx asked.

"Elias just called in reinforcements. Even at full strength I couldn't take forty of those advanced thralls. And if I could, I'd have no strength left to deal with Elias. I hope the boss has a brilliant idea because I don't. Not yet anyway."

He refocused on the thralls. They were spreading out in a loose formation around the building. No sneaking in through the ground floor now. But maybe they could find another way.

"Ruq, fly over the building and see if it has a roof access."

The view shifted as Ruq glided over it. Sure enough, he spotted an open doorway up there. Daisuke could easily fly over the thralls and then work his way down. Not that there was any point until he had a way to deal with Elias, but he felt better having some sort of plan.

He was just about to resume his search for a resting place when his phone buzzed. "Boss?"

"How are things there?"

"Well, it could be worse." He filled her in on the situation. "My current plan is to bypass the thralls and go in through the roof. We just need a method to deal with Elias. How's that going?"

"Donny has the journal and is, I assume, working diligently. I'm going to reach out to my contacts in the Cairo police department and get them to issue a lockdown order for the campus. That way you won't have to worry about any civilians showing up."

"That would be a huge help, boss, thanks. I'll keep an eye on things. As long as Elias doesn't try anything, I'm content to let matters stand as they are. Did Helena make it home?"

"I haven't heard from her, but I assume so. I said she didn't need to come in until morning."

"Hopefully she's enjoying a well-earned rest. I'm certainly looking forward to one of my own when this mess is sorted out."

"You'll have earned it. I'll be in touch as soon as Donny figures it out."

She disconnected and Daisuke sighed. Having to rely on others sucked, but that's what it meant to be part of a team, and heaven knew he wasn't the one to research a complex magical formula. At least not in a hurry.

He spotted a nearby park bench and walked over. Not exactly the most comfortable resting place he could imagine, but under these circumstances it was about the most beautiful sight he'd seen in days.

Elias leaned on the workbench in his lab. He thought he'd been weary before, but after summoning so many thralls, he felt hollowed out in a way he'd never experienced. Umbral Tide was a greater demon, for goodness' sake, he shouldn't be this weak. Did he do something wrong during the binding process?

No! Elias had spent half his life working on the spell circle which fused them. The process was perfect. Whatever went wrong, that hadn't been the cause.

In the back of his mind the demon's amusement mingled with contempt.

Elias ground his teeth for a moment then forced himself to relax. Demons were, by their nature, cruel, arrogant things. Its thoughts meant nothing. He was in charge. Umbral Tide was nothing more than a power source, a corrupt battery for Elias to use as he saw fit.

Thankfully it was a rechargeable battery. The demon's strength had already begun returning, albeit far too slowly for Elias's liking.

Much as he hated asking, he swallowed his pride and said, "Is there no way for me to recover more quickly?"

There is, but you lack the necessary sacrifices. If you had a hundred or so prisoners, you could kill them and feed off their pain and life force. That would do wonders to restore my strength. We should've fled this area and harvested a small town. I would've been fully recovered by now.

Elias snarled. "Your power is mine now. You need to hammer that into whatever serves as your brain. Stop thinking of yourself as a separate being."

No reply from the demon. Well, that was fine. Whether the creature accepted it or not was irrelevant. It could do nothing beyond what Elias wished.

He staggered over to the wall and slid down to sit on the floor. Though it was far from dignified, right now he didn't care and besides, no one could see him anyways. His enemies had no hope of getting through so many thralls. He had all the time he needed to regain his strength.

And once he did, he'd be free to resume sacrificing this city to Astaroth.

CHAPTER TWENTY-FIVE

Daisuke's phone rang, bringing him out of a doze. He wasn't sure how long he'd been sitting on the park bench. It remained pitch black out, so not that long. As he reached for his phone he caught a glimpse of Jinx's little frown out of the corner of his eye. It was sweet of her to worry, but he'd done stuff like this enough times that he'd gotten used to exhaustion. More importantly, when he reached for the ether, he felt mostly recovered.

He pulled his phone out. It read four in the morning. He'd managed a few hours' rest, not too bad.

"Tell me you have good news, boss."

"As a matter of fact, I do. Donny said the process of reversing the bonding was straight forward. There were a lot of technical details I won't bore you with, but suffice it to say we know how to separate them. Donny prepared a reverse spell circle. All you need to do is charge it with ether and picture the circle appearing beneath Elias. The magic will do the rest."

"Sounds simple. That's good given how worn out I am. Is

it okay if I send Jinx to pick up the scroll? I don't want to waste any power I don't have to."

"That's fine. I also got through to my contact in the police department. They sent an emergency text citywide warning everyone to shelter in place until further notice."

"That's one problem sorted at least. I'll be in touch once things are settled."

"Good luck, Daisuke."

He disconnected and turned to Jinx. "Do you mind shadow walking to base and picking up that scroll? I kind of volunteered you without asking."

"It's no problem. Whatever I can do to relieve some of the burden, I'm happy to do. Be back in a minute." She got up and vanished into a shadow, leaving him alone.

He focused on his connection to Ruq. "What are the thralls up to?"

Nothing. They're just milling around outside. The stupid things give demons a bad name.

"Demons already have a bad name. No change on the roof access?"

Still clear. You really think whatever magic the cellar dweller came up with is going to work?

Daisuke stood and stretched. Sitting on the hard bench had left him a bit stiff. "Donny might not be the most personable fellow, but he knows his magic. If he says it'll work, I'm confident it will. Of course, if I'm wrong, we'll need to get out of there in a hurry."

Assuming we can. Elias is liable to have something to say about it.

"No doubt. We'll just have to do what we always do."

Make it up as we go and hope it works out?

Daisuke grinned. "Exactly."

He sensed Jinx a moment before she emerged from the shadow paths. She'd changed out of her civilian clothes and into her shadow-silk dress. If that wasn't a sight to motivate a man to survive, he didn't know what was. She held a rolled-up scroll in her hand.

"Here you go."

"Thanks." He took the scroll and unrolled it. A ludicrously complex spell circle covered the surface. If Donny drew that in three hours he was better than Daisuke thought. "Why the change of clothes?"

"I didn't want anything to interfere with my magic, even a tiny bit. Plus, if I need to hide in a shadow, I'll be able to now. That should save you a bit of strength when we fly to the roof."

"It certainly should. And speaking of, I'd say it's time to get this show on the road. I'll need you to hold off the thralls while I'm fighting Elias."

"I can help you."

"You will be helping me," Daisuke said. "He's going to call his guards as soon as he senses my arrival. I can't fight him and them at the same time. I need you to handle this. Okay?"

She hesitated then nodded. "I'll do my best."

Daisuke stepped closer and gave her a hug. "I know you will, but no matter what, take care of yourself. This isn't a win if one of us dies in the process. If you need to run for it, then run."

"I will," she said in a tone which made it clear she totally wouldn't.

He gently lifted her chin to force her to look into his eyes. "I'm serious. If you don't promise to look after yourself, and mean it, I won't be able to focus on the fight. So promise me."

Jinx blew out a long breath. "I promise."

"Good." He leaned in and kissed her. "Now let's do this."

Jinx vanished into his shadow and Daisuke cast the spell that concealed his life force followed by a flying spell. He soared straight up then turned toward where he sensed Ruq. His familiar joined him as he passed, gliding along at his shoulder.

A few seconds later he landed on the roof. Nothing magical happened and no monsters attacked them. He'd been somewhat concerned about an unpleasant surprise waiting for them and was pleased to be wrong.

"I did check the place over," Ruq said. "I wouldn't miss something obvious."

"I know. It's not the obvious things that worried me." Daisuke strode over to the door, or more accurately, the door frame—someone had ripped the door itself off its hinges and tossed it aside—and checked it for traps. Once again everything came up clean. "I'm not sure if he's careless, stupid, or arrogant."

"He's a demon worshipper," Ruq said. "Arrogant is always a safe bet."

Daisuke couldn't argue with Ruq's assessment.

He descended the stairs as quickly as he could while maintaining some semblance of stealth. Fortunately the building wasn't especially tall and he soon reached the ground floor. He activated his tracking spell and it led away from the entrance.

"Jinx." She emerged from his shadow. "This is where we part company. The front doors are down this hall. Just go straight and you'll come right to them. Elias is deeper inside."

She nodded. "See you soon."

He grinned. "Better believe it."

Daisuke jogged off down another hall and did his best to

put Jinx out of his mind. They both had their own jobs to do. She couldn't help him and he had to trust that she could handle hers.

A couple of twists and turns later and he stood at the entrance to a storage room. The spell indicated that Elias was under here somewhere. Finding the entrance would be the trick. A bit of concentration refined the tracking spell, making it more focused.

He swept the staff back and forth like a metal detector, and near the back wall found a passage under the floor, but no obvious way to open it. There had to be a trick to it, but he didn't have time to search.

Earth magic would serve here. He tapped the staff on the floor and a rumble shook the room. Metal and stone twisted and collapsed with a horrible crash, revealing a set of steps leading into the earth.

"Think he heard us?" Ruq asked.

Daisuke ignored the question and slipped the Elemental Orb out of his satchel. With that he descended into the basement, picking his way around the debris as he went. At the bottom he found another workshop lit by creepy greenish flames. Why in the world demon worshippers wanted their lighting to have a gangrenous tint was beyond him, but it seemed popular.

Elias stood in the center of the room looking even more sunken and undead than before. "Why must you struggle so? It would be so much easier for you to just surrender to your fate. You'd have no fears, or concerns—"

"No free will."

"Free will is overrated. All it does is cause problems. I'll give you one chance to submit. You've proven yourself a capable foe. Join me and I'll make you my second-in-command."

"I already have a job and it's killing you."

"Then die like the fool you are!" Elias threw his hand forward.

Darkness roared out in a wave at Daisuke, who countered by raising the Elemental Orb. It sucked up all the power while protecting him from harm. He let out a breath he hadn't realized he was holding. Despite his confidence, he'd harbored doubts about his plan until that moment.

When the torrent of corruption ended, Elias was standing there staring at his hand in disbelief. He shifted his gaze to Daisuke. "You're supposed to be dead."

"I assumed that was the idea. Happy to disappoint. Want to try again?"

Something snapped in Elias. Daisuke could see it on his face. His eyes narrowed and his expression twisted into something insane. That was the only way he could describe it.

Elias threw both hands forward and loosed an even greater burst of corruption.

This was it. Daisuke had to drain him dry to give the spell circle any chance to work. He willed the orb to absorb all the corruption and to keep pulling when it started to abate. It sucked everything up until only a few wisps clung to Elias's fingertips.

The professor had gone from mad to forlorn. He looked all around as if uncertain where he was and what had happened. Daisuke found the whole thing too pathetic.

Daisuke swapped the orb for the scroll and unrolled it.

"What are you doing now?" Elias asked, his voice despondent.

Daisuke ignored the question and channeled ether into the spell circle. When the whole design was glowing he willed it to appear under Elias. The magic responded. The circle vanished from the scroll and reappeared on the floor, surrounding Elias.

The professor howled and thrashed as the magic ripped liquid darkness out of his body.

The process wasn't pretty. Plenty of blood came along with the demon's form. While the spell did its thing, Daisuke tossed the now-useless scroll away and grabbed Umbral Tide's prison. He set it on the floor and got ready for round two with the demon.

Jinx watched Daisuke until he'd moved out of sight then took off down the hall toward the entrance. No matter what, she swore she wouldn't let a single one of those thralls reach him.

The entry area looked like plenty of others she'd visited lately and she got busy dragging sofas and chairs up against the door to serve as a barrier. She doubted they'd slow the thralls by much, but today every second counted. Outside, the thralls visible through the door paid her not the least attention. She wasn't exactly being quiet with her work, but they kept staring out toward the city. They really were remarkably stupid.

When she'd piled up every piece of furniture not nailed to the floor, Jinx considered what else she could do to slow them. As she considered her options, the thralls turned as one and surged toward the door. She knew what that meant. The fight downstairs must've begun.

The lead thralls grabbed the doors and pulled, yanking them back and forth as they fought to break the lock. Others pounded on the frame and casing. All the while they roared and moaned like the damned things they were.

As she feared, it didn't take long for them to breach the doors. The hinges gave way with an awful shriek then the thralls were pushing through, shoving the furniture aside as if it weighed nothing. Stupid they might be, but they lacked nothing in the muscle department.

Jinx shot bursts of dark flames, trying to burn their hands and faces where she had a clear shot. Shadow webs would do nothing against these corrupt things. Demons of any sort, but especially undead-based ones, were a bad matchup for her. Her efforts bought her maybe a minute then the thralls came running toward her.

The entry area was too wide for her to fight them so Jinx fell back to the hall where they were at least forced to come at her three at a time. Still not ideal, but better than getting surrounded.

As soon as the hall narrowed she slowed and started blasting. She aimed for their knees in the hope of slowing them down. Unfortunately they resisted her magic and even when she did some damage, one of the other thralls smashed the injured one aside and took its place.

She turned down the hall Daisuke had taken, the thralls only yards behind her. This time Jinx threw up a wall of fire. Her magic was so depleted the thralls pushed right through it, barely singed.

Pitiful. Nothing she did even slowed them down.

An open door a little ways further on caught her eye. That had to be where he went in. The doorway was the narrowest place she expected to find. She had to stop them there or she wasn't stopping them at all.

Jinx darted away, ducked through the opening, and spun around, ready to fight to her last breath.

The thralls stopped outside. The vacant look was back in their eyes. She had just time enough to wonder what in the world was going on now when some invisible force ripped the corruption burning on their chests out and dragged it down a hole in the floor behind her. In a few minutes, all the thralls had collapsed.

She was safe, for the moment at least.

CHAPTER TWENTY-SIX

Daisuke's grip on the Staff of Law tightened as the flow of darkness rushing out of Elias slowed. It wouldn't be long before Umbral Tide was free. The moment it was, Daisuke had to act quickly. He absolutely couldn't allow the demon to make its escape. He had to prevent that no matter what.

With a final spurt of blood, the last of the demon emerged from Elias's back.

"Umbral Tide! By my blood and the power of the staff you are bound. Freeze!"

The writhing darkness went still, offering almost no resistance. For a demon this powerful that seemed impossible. Daisuke immediately suspected a trap.

There is no trap, mortal. The fool who bound me used up my power thinking it inexhaustible. I couldn't fight your imp right now.

That was convenient. "By my will and the power of the seal be bound. By the blood of Solomon and might of the Staff of Law, Umbral Tide be bound in bronze."

The demon's form rushed into the bronze urn. Daisuke focused hard, drawing the scattered bits in as well. That should take care of the thrall problem upstairs. The entire process was silent. Of all the bindings he'd done, none had been odder than this. Usually the demons howled and raged as they were dragged in by ethereal chains. Umbral Tide went in as obediently as a well-trained dog going into its crate at bedtime.

I am weary of humans. Dealing with Elias's stupidity left me longing for a thousand years of oblivion. Perhaps the next time I'm freed, it will be by less of a fool.

Daisuke never broke his focus, but he couldn't help thinking that anyone dumb enough to free a demon couldn't be a terribly wise person in the first place.

When he sensed no more of the demon remained free, Daisuke cast the final spell. "Darkness bound in bronze, blood compels and the staff commands, be sealed away for all time."

A new cap formed, sealing the urn. At last Umbral Tide's symbol appeared in the center. And it was done. Even without major resistance, the binding took a toll on his already weary body. Hopefully the next emergency would hold off for at least a week.

He bent to pick up the urn. There were few things he wanted more than to collect Jinx and head for home.

A pained shout had him spinning, a spell at the ready.

Professor Elias lay on the ground, knife in hand and Ruq perched on his unmoving chest.

"He tried to sneak up on you," Ruq said. "Considering how much blood he lost, I'm impressed he could even move."

"Good job. Is there anything here we need to grab before the locals show up?"

“Nah, it’s all junk and cult propaganda. Nothing we need taking up space on our table.”

Daisuke grunted and picked up the urn. They certainly had enough junk on their table. Using the staff as a walking stick, Daisuke headed for the stairs. He barely reached the debris field when Jinx came rushing down to meet him.

“Are you okay?” they asked at the same time.

“I’m fine.” Again in stereo.

They stared at each other then started laughing. It was the laughter that followed surviving something you weren’t sure you would. It felt good at the same time his ill-used body complained about the shaking.

When he caught his breath Daisuke sent the boss a text saying they were on their way back. That done, he turned to Jinx. “Let’s get out of here.”

EPILOGUE

"So, I took Jinx home, dropped Umbral Tide off in the vault and came here." Daisuke sat sprawled in the chair facing Angelique. He looked exhausted, hardly a surprise given it was nearly five in the morning. "I figured the locals could handle whatever else needed handling given that I sorted out the demon situation."

She could barely make out what he was saying.

Daisuke waved a hand in front of her eyes. "Boss? You in there?"

Angelique gave a full-body shudder. "Yes, I'm fine. Good work on this one. Why don't you go home and get some sleep."

He cocked his head, a little frown creasing his lips. "When's the last time you went home and rested?"

"I don't need to sleep."

"That's not what I asked. Sleep or not, even you need to decompress eventually. I've never seen you space out like that during a debriefing. You were a million miles away."

She wanted to snap at him to mind his own business. That reaction as much as anything told her how close to the edge she was. Nevertheless, she had so much to do. "I'll be fine."

Daisuke shook his head and stood. "Nonsense. I'll take you home so you can rest. At least until noon. Come on."

She stared at him but he clearly wasn't joking. "What if something happens? I can't be out of touch for half a day."

He picked her cellphone up off the desk and wiggled it between his thumb and forefinger. "This thing works anywhere in the city. That's kind of the point of having one. If one of the team needs something they can call or text. Now ups-a-daisy."

He held out his hand and she reluctantly took it. Angelique couldn't believe she was letting him talk her into this. "I don't think sitting alone in my apartment will be any more restful than staying here."

"Alone?" Daisuke led her out of her office and outside. "I'm staying with you. Otherwise you're apt to come right back here as soon as I drop you off."

Heat spread through her. How long had it been since she'd been alone with a man? It spoke volumes that she couldn't remember. A century at least. "I'm not sleeping with you."

"I can't believe I'm going to say this, but I'm so tired I'm not even thinking about that. It's a rare event, let me tell you. I should be up for it later though if you change your mind." He waggled his eyebrows at her and grinned.

She smiled despite herself and some of the accumulated tension melted away.

Daisuke flagged down a cab and she gave the driver the

address of her apartment building. When she did Daisuke whistled. "That neighborhood isn't cheap. Maybe I should ask for a raise."

"You can ask."

He laughed again. Such a free and open sound. It did her spirit good to hear it.

They reached the steel-and-glass building and took the elevator up to her floor. They didn't encounter a soul on the way. At this time of day, all sensible mortals were asleep. When they reached her front door, she realized she didn't have her key. It was in the drawer of the desk in her office. Her cheeks warmed as embarrassment flooded through her. Why such a simple thing embarrassed her she couldn't have said.

"I forgot my key."

"No worries, boss." He popped the lock with a spell and guided her inside with a gentle hand on her back. When he flipped the light on, he whistled again. "Very nice indeed. You could fit three of my apartments in here."

The space was immaculate. As well it should be given how little time she spent here.

"Okay, where's the bedroom?"

"Daisuke..." She put a bit of a warning in her tone.

"Relax, boss. We need to get you settled then I'm going to borrow your shower."

She sighed and surrendered. "The door to your right."

Once again he led the way. The queen-sized bed was neatly made. Another door led to the master bathroom. Daisuke ignored them both and went to her dresser. He went through two drawers then brightened.

"Here we go, pajamas. Brand new if I'm not mistaken." He

handed her a pair of blue satin shorts and a matching chemise. "You get comfy while I wash up."

So saying he strode off into the bathroom. The water started running a moment later.

She stared at the shimmering outfit. Was she really going to do this? Angelique hadn't taken orders from anyone since getting cast out of Heaven. Why was she letting Daisuke talk her into something she didn't want to do?

A little sigh slipped out. Because she did want to. In fact, she needed to rest. She'd known she needed to for weeks but kept putting it off. Daisuke was just serving as an excuse to do what she knew she needed to.

"Ruq, are you here?"

The answer came a moment later when the living room TV came on. Daisuke did say the imp liked to watch infomercials. She closed and locked the bedroom door just to be safe and stripped out of her familiar gray suit. For a moment she felt like a knight removing a suit of armor. With just the pajamas on, work Angelique, the one all her people called boss, vanished.

Only the real her, a fallen angel too corrupt to live in Heaven, remained. Was that what he would see? The thought of Daisuke looking at her like one of the monsters he fought bothered her more than she would ever acknowledge.

The water stopped and she hurried over to slide under the covers. A few minutes later he emerged from the bathroom and slid into bed beside her. Angelique stiffened but after a few seconds of nothing happening relaxed again. A faint stirring of the ether and the bedroom light switched off. The only light came from her glowing eyes.

"Close your eyes." Daisuke gently stroked her hair. "I'm

here. I'll stay as long as you need to rest. There's nothing you need to worry about. Just relax."

Angelique took a deep breath and let her back press against his chest. He felt warm and strong. Daisuke slipped his arm around her.

At last Angelique closed her eyes, confident everything really would be okay.

AUTHOR NOTE

Hello everyone,

I hope you enjoyed Daisuke's adventure in Egypt. It was a lot of fun to write and now I'm looking forward to his next adventure.

An adventure that will take him Caribbean. The land of Voodoo, Hoodoo, and all kinds of weird shit. If you recognize that quote email me and tell me where it's from.

You can sign up for my newsletter at www.jamesewisher.com. and be the first to know when the knew books come out.

As always, thanks for reading.

James E Wisher

ALSO BY JAMES E. WISHER

The 72 Demons

The Blood of Solomon

A Friend in Need

The Demon Masks

Hunt For The Devil Man

A Family Reunion

The Cursed Fortress

The Aegis of Merlin:

The Impossible Wizard

The Awakening

The Chimera Jar

The Raven's Shadow

Escape From the Dragon Czar

Wrath of the Dragon Czar

The Four Nations Tournament

Death Incarnate

Atlantis Rising

Rise of the Demon Lords

The Pale Princess

Malice

Hearts of Corrupt Fire

Ultima Thule

Aegis of Merlin Omnibus Vol 1.

Aegis of Merlin Omnibus Vol 2.

The Complete Aegis of Merlin Omnibus

Summoned to Another Words and Forced to Fight The Demon King

The Summoned Hero

The Birth of Ronin

The Fate of The Five Kingdoms

The Plague Lands

Elfhome

The Immortal Apprentice Trilogy

The War With Audin (Prequel Novella)

The Hunt For Revenge

The Army of Darkness

The Apprentice Reborn

The Soul Bound Saga

An Unwelcome Journey

Darkness in Tiber

Depths of Betrayal

The Black Iron Empire

Overmage

The Divine Key Trilogy

Shadow Magic

For The Greater Good

The Divine Key Awakens

The Portal Wars Saga

The Hidden Tower

The Great Northern War

The Portal Thieves

The Master of Magic

The Chamber of Eternity

The Heart of Alchemy

The Sanguine Scroll

Shadow of The Dragons

The Dragonspire Chronicles

The Black Egg

The Mysterious Coin

The Dragons' Graveyard

The Slave War

The Sunken Tower

The Dragon Empress

The Dragonspire Chronicles Omnibus Vol. 1

The Dragonspire Chronicles Omnibus Vol. 2

The Complete Dragonspire Chronicles Omnibus

Soul Force Saga

Disciples of the Horned One Trilogy:

Darkness Rising

Raging Sea and Trembling Earth

Harvest of Souls

Disciples of the Horned One Omnibus

Chains of the Fallen Arc:

Dreaming in the Dark

On Blackened Wings

Chains of the Fallen Omnibus

The Complete Soul Force Saga Omnibus

Other Fantasy Novels:

The Squire

Death and Honor Omnibus

The Rogue Star Series:

Children of Darkness

Children of the Void

Children of Junk

Rogue Star Omnibus Vol. 1

Children of the Black Ship

Children of The End

ABOUT THE AUTHOR

James E. Wisher is a writer of science fiction and Fantasy novels. He's been writing since high school and reading everything he could get his hands on for as long as he can remember.

www.ingramcontent.com/pod-product-compliance
Lightning Source LLC
LaVergne TN
LVHW090942080826
845145LV00003B/858

* 9 7 8 1 6 8 5 2 0 1 2 8 9 *